SURVIVAL

CLOVERDALE – BOOK TWO

BRUNO MILLER

SURVIVAL:
Cloverdale, Book Two

Copyright © 2019 Bruno Miller

All rights reserved. No part of this book may be reproduced in any form or by any electronic or mechanical means, including information storage and retrieval systems—except in the case of brief quotations embodied in critical articles or reviews—without permission in writing from the author.

This book is a work of fiction. The characters, events, and places portrayed in this book are products of the author's imagination and are either fictitious or are used fictitiously. Any similarity to real person, living or dead, is purely coincidental and not intended by the author.

Find out when Bruno's next book is coming out.
Join his mailing list for release news, sales, and the occasional survival tip. No spam ever.
http://brunomillerauthor.com/sign-up/

Published in the United States of America.

Would you survive?

Vince Walker and the remaining survivors from the town of Cloverdale, Indiana continue to come to terms with their new reality. Accepting the fact that the country has been thrust into nuclear war with an unknown enemy means they must forget their former lives and forge ahead.

The affects of the EMP blasts have left the survivors with no utilities, and no communication with the world outside of their once sleepy little town. A power surge also resulted in widespread fires, destroying most buildings and homes, leaving few resources intact.

The challenge of living is made even tougher by a roving gang of looters that will stop at nothing short of killing Vince and his crew in order to take what few supplies remain.

Can they outlast their enemies? Or will the fight for survival become their last stand?

Other Books by Bruno Miller

The Dark Road Series

Breakdown

Escape

Resistance

Fallout

Extraction

Cloverdale Series

Impact

· 1 ·

Vince rubbed his eyes as he tried to come to terms with what Mary was telling him. Were the looters really back already? Why hadn't the person on watch blown the horn? Or did he, but Vince was just sleeping too hard to hear it? The last thing he remembered was scratching Nugget's head and waiting for Mary to come out of the bathroom. He felt like he had only been out for a few minutes, not nearly long enough to get any rest.

"What should we do?" Mary asked, interrupting his thoughts as he struggled to shake off the sleepiness that overwhelmed him.

"Are the others up?" Vince asked. If the looters were back, they would need everyone on deck and ready to fight.

"Cy was going to check in on everyone and make sure they were up," Mary answered. Nugget whined at the door as the sound of footsteps moved past the room outside. In the dim light,

Vince struggled to make out the time on his watch as the beam from Mary's flashlight bounced around the room. He was disappointed to see that it was three in the morning. Vince had hoped that the overindulgence in alcohol would eventually put the looters out of commission for the night and buy them some time. He was at least expecting his people to have the night for some much-needed rest and maybe have a chance to organize themselves in the morning before another attack.

"Hey, you should probably turn that light off," Vince said. Then it dawned on him that the others probably had their flashlights going as well. The looters knew their location, but that didn't mean they needed to advertise which rooms they were in. He quickly pulled on his boots, realizing that he needed to take control of things before any more mistakes were made.

He grabbed the shotgun leaning next to the bed and used it to push himself up to his feet. The soreness in his back and muscles was a painful reminder of what they had endured yesterday. And now it was starting all over again and much too soon.

"Wait here while I find out what's going on," Vince said.

"Be careful." Mary pulled Nugget back from the door as Vince reattached his holster and tucked the .45 back into it.

Vince nodded. "I'll be back as soon as I can. Make sure your shotgun is loaded and ready for action."

"It is," Mary confirmed.

Once outside the room, Vince was greeted with the strong smell of smoke and what he thought was burned rubber. Reminded of how overwhelming the thick air was, he pulled his T-shirt up over his face. He had loaned his makeshift mask to Tom but couldn't remember what he had done with the extra hardware store masks. But there was no time to worry about that now.

He glanced down the covered walkway that ran in front of the motel rooms, looking for any signs of activity. Sure enough, just as he had suspected, he could see traces of light bleeding through the thin curtains from inside the rooms. The large windows that faced the road would give away their location. He knocked on the first door next to his and Mary's room and was greeted almost immediately by a clearly excited Bill. Bill stepped outside and was about to close the door, but Vince stopped him. "Tell your wife to turn off the flashlight or at least keep it down low."

Bill leaned back into the room and relayed the message before closing the door and joining Vince outside. "I saw headlights coming from that direction." Bill pointed toward the interstate.

Vince couldn't make out anything through the thick smoke. He was disappointed to see the smoke hadn't thinned any since he'd last been outside. Of course, he wasn't surprised or expecting it to improve much; it had only been a few hours and there were numerous fires still raging in the distance.

"How many?" Vince asked.

"I only saw one set, but it's hard to tell with all the smoke. I beeped the horn as soon as I saw them and then went door to door, waking people up." Bill clutched his rifle in both hands.

"You did good. I need you to take your position back in the truck and honk the horn if you see them again. I'll go check on the others and get them into position," Vince said.

"Okay, Major." Bill headed back to the truck as Vince moved on to the Morgans' room. He was about to knock when Reese cracked the door open and did her best to hold Buster back. She looked tired—and understandably so. She rubbed her eyes as she tried to block the doorway with her legs. Buster managed to force his nose through the small opening and sniffed wildly at the outside air.

"My dad's coming. Just getting his shoes on." Reese struggled to keep Buster from gaining any more ground.

"Okay, tell him to meet us at the truck. You and your mom stay in the room and keep your flashlights off, okay?"

"Okay. I'll tell him." She grabbed Buster's

collar and pulled him back but stopped before closing the door. "Are those same people back?" she asked.

"I'm not sure, but just to be safe, lock yourselves in after your dad leaves."

"Okay." She sighed and disappeared behind the door.

Heavy footsteps came from ahead before Cy and Tom appeared out of the smoke. They had come from the parking lot and were moving fast. Just then, Bill blew the truck horn twice, and Vince could hear him get out and slam the door.

"Someone's coming," Cy huffed as he and Tom came to a sudden stop near Vince.

"Looks like just one vehicle," Tom added.

Bill appeared and joined the group. "What do we do?"

Vince looked at their faces as he thought about the best course of action. It seemed strange that there was only one car this time. If anything, he expected even more of the looters to show up and to bring everything they had. After the last incident, the looters wouldn't want to take any chances. Vince was beginning to think this was someone else, but there was no way of knowing for sure and no reason to let his guard down.

"We need to split up," Vince said. "If there's going to be another gunfight, we need to draw their fire away from the motel. Bill, I want you at the south corner of the property. Not too far. Find a place to hide where you can see the parking lot and the rooms." Vince pointed to the far end of the motel.

"What about us?" Tom asked.

"You two, come with me." Vince started for the opposite corner of the motel property, looking back to make sure Cy and Tom were following close behind. Now that he thought about it, he regretted not setting up some type of roadblock. Even if it didn't stop the looters and they drove around the obstacle, it would have given Vince and his people a defensible position ahead of the motel and a chance to cut them off before they got too close. He was disappointed with himself for not thinking about that sooner, but he chalked it up to being exhausted and tried to focus on what he was going to do now.

He stopped at the corner of the motel office and looked around. There were two large dumpsters along the side of the building, and he directed Cy to take up a position behind them. From there, he would have a clear line of sight to the road that led in from the interstate, and the AR-15 would have the range needed to make an effective shot from that distance.

"Cy," Vince said.

"Yeah, Dad?"

"Don't hesitate to shoot. These people mean

business. They're killers. Remember that," Vince cautioned. Cy acknowledged his warning with a quick nod before turning and heading off toward the dumpsters. Vince never imagined he'd be giving his son instructions to shoot at people, not in his wildest dreams. But here he was, doing just that.

Vince and Tom continued to the edge of the road and made their way into the drainage ditch that ran along the edge of North Main. It wasn't very deep, but in the darkness and if they went prone, it would conceal them—at least long enough so they could get the jump on whoever was coming. It would also get them close enough for the shotguns to be effective.

Vince could see the headlights now as he and Tom crouched down and moved along the ditch bank. Vince stopped behind a utility box and decided it was a good place for Tom to hide.

"You stay here. I'm going a little farther down to that telephone pole. You still have the slugs I gave you?"

Tom pulled them out of his shirt pocket and held them out.

"Good, load them in your gun and be ready to back me up." Vince turned and continued forward, making sure to keep a low profile as he went. Moving like this hurt his back, but the vehicle was close now and he didn't want to risk being seen. He crouched on the ground when he reached the pole and laid the shotgun down next to him.

Vince glanced back down the ditch and saw that Tom was ready as well. Nothing to do now but wait and see who this was.

· 2 ·

As the vehicle drew closer, Vince could make out the round headlights, and for a moment, he thought it was a Jeep. But as the small SUV emerged from the dense smoke and took shape, Vince recognized the square outline of John Rice's '75 Ford box-top Bronco and the unmistakable baby blue paint job and white hard top.

Vince rose from the ground as quickly as his aching body would allow and walked onto the road in front of the approaching vehicle. He waved his arms and the shotgun over his head as a sense of dread came over him. What if it wasn't John? What if someone had taken his truck? Maybe he should have let the vehicle pass before giving up his hiding spot, just in case.

But it was too late now. He was in the headlights, and whether it was John or not, he'd been spotted for sure. The old Bronco's brakes squealed as it came to a stop several feet in front of

Vince. The door opened, and Vince was relieved to see John step out and approach him.

"Major, is that you?" John asked.

Vince met a dirty and tired John at the front of the truck. "It's me all right. You have no idea how glad I am to see you."

"The feeling is mutual." John let out a heavy sigh, and instead of their usual stiff handshake, John embraced Vince with a hug and hung on to him for a second. It was then that Vince knew something was wrong. He could see by the expression on John's face that he was struggling to keep it together. He thought it was strange that John was alone but initially dismissed the concern, hoping that his wife and kids were somewhere safe and that John had left them behind while he ventured out. But Vince's gut told him something different, and he didn't have the nerve to ask John if they were all right.

John let go of Vince and stepped back as Tom approached them from his hiding spot behind the utility box.

John started shaking his head, and Vince knew the answer to the question he'd been reluctant to ask.

"It's all gone." John sniffed and wiped at his eyes. "Carroll, the house, my life, everything. It's all gone. The house was engulfed in flames by the time I got there. There was nothing I could do." He looked down at the ground as Tom walked up to where they were standing.

"It's good to see you, John. We thought it was the looters coming back for round two," Tom said.

"Looters?" John cleared his throat and struggled to regain his composure.

"Yeah, we had a run-in with a group that came from the interstate in cars and four-wheelers. They were going to clean my place out, and we got into a gunfight with them." Vince paused and glanced back at Tom before continuing. "They shot Jim from the motel. He didn't make it."

John shook his head in disgust. "I can't believe it's come to this already."

"We managed to get a few of them. The bodies are in the field out behind my shop if you want to take a look," Vince said.

"No point in that. I've seen enough for one day and I'm exhausted. I had to drive all the way around town and come up the interstate. The streets are a mess and impassable right now. With all the buildings collapsed, there's debris all over the roads. I didn't want to risk it and blow the tires out on the truck." John looked back at the Bronco, and as he faced the headlights, Vince could see just how exhausted and dirty he looked.

"Why don't we head over to the motel? We're all holding up there until things settle down," Vince said.

"Or longer," Tom added.

"How many survivors?" John asked.

Vince shook his head. "So far, there are twelve of us. We tried to look for more, but we couldn't get through. The smoke was too thick. Mary and I nearly got trapped over on Lewis Avenue. It got pretty hairy over there in the older section of town, and on top of everything else there were a lot of gas tanks going off like bombs. It's like a war zone in town. Maybe worse."

Tom shrugged. "I haven't heard any explosions for a while now."

"Yeah, but there are still plenty of fires burning out there," John said. "It probably won't be safe to venture back into town for another day or so at least."

"Why don't you come back to the motel with us and we'll get you set up in one of the rooms," Vince said. "You look like you could use some rest."

"Yeah, I could," John agreed.

John offered Vince and Tom a ride back to the motel in his truck, but when he saw the back seat of the Bronco, Tom said he would walk back. John had managed to salvage a few things from his squad car and the shed at his house, all of which was stuffed into the back seat. Vince was glad to see a few two-way radios among the gear.

As Vince and John made their way back to the motel, Vince tried to give John a quick rundown on their situation and who was staying at the motel.

He also filled him in on his thoughts about getting the power back up and running and offered to take him over to the garage so he could clean up a little, but John seemed distant and said he'd rather just get to the motel.

Vince was once again reminded of how lucky he was to have his son with him, safe and sound—and also how unfortunate so many others were to have lost it all. He wanted to tell John about his plans and thoughts for the coming days but restrained himself in an effort not to overwhelm him with information. There would be time for all that later. Right now, John needed rest and a chance to process all that had happened.

When they pulled into the motel parking lot, a small group of survivors met them. Mary led the pack. She was the first one to him and had her arms open. She embraced John without hesitation and held on to him for a while. Tom had reached the motel before them by cutting through the grass and had obviously informed the others of John's situation.

He struggled to keep it together as Mary finally released him and stepped back so the others could say hello.

Cy approached next and already had a room key in his hand.

"Good to see you again, Cy." John shook his hand. "Wish it was under better circumstances."

Cy nodded and handed him the room key. "Glad you're here with us. You're in 106, right next to me."

The others came over in turn and said hello and offered their condolences. Everybody chipped in and unloaded the gear from his truck. Once finished, one by one they began dispersing to their rooms, trying to salvage what was left of the night and get some much-needed rest.

Vince and Mary hung out for a while in John's room and brought over their container of water to share with him while he settled in as best as he could. They listened to John describe what he had seen and encountered in his travels, although it was nothing new or different than what they had witnessed.

Vince accepted the fact that it would be another day or more before they could venture into town and attempt to salvage anything usable. He also realized that the hope of finding any more survivors was slim. Even though they had seen it all with their own eyes, hearing John's description of town made clear the reality of the situation once more and reminded them that they were on their own. Survival depended on them and their ability to adapt to this harsh new world.

· 3 ·

The time passed painfully slow over the next couple of days, and at times, it seemed to stand still as everyone sat in their rooms. Playing cards for matchsticks and staring out the window, hoping for rain, grew old fast. The only relief for Vince was the short trips he and Cy made to the garage, where they refilled the water containers and gathered food. But they didn't dare linger any longer than necessary over there in case the looters came back and caught them. As much as he would have liked to start working on a power supply for the motel using the solar electric system at the garage, he knew it wasn't the time yet. He also didn't want to risk using too much of the stored power. The sun hadn't fully broken through the thick smoke and he doubted the solar panels had been able to generate much power. He wanted to save what energy there was to operate the well pump. Without clean water, they wouldn't make it.

The smoke remained thick—another reason to put off doing any real work outdoors. The other day, they had all braved it long enough to dig a shallow grave and bury Jim's body. Even though they kept it brief and only said a few words out of respect for Jim, they were almost all coughing uncontrollably and barely finished the job. They were forced to cut it short and take shelter indoors.

Even during daylight hours, the darkness and stench of burnt things hung over them as a constant reminder that their situation was still beyond their control. It was too early to venture into town, and at this point, any trip would only yield disappointment and the risk of injury.

Taking a full breath of air without the use of a mask remained nearly impossible and always brought on a fit of coughing. Reese's mother, Hannah, and Tom and Beverly's boy, Ryan, were just beginning to recover from smoke inhalation, and Vince didn't see the need to put anybody else's health at risk until things settled down. Despite their best efforts to stay out of the smoke-laden air, they had all developed a bit of a cough and spoke with a now familiar raspy tone. If it wasn't for the water and food they were able to gather from his garage, Vince wasn't sure if they would have made it through this first couple of days at all. He also knew the snacks and protein bars they were eating weren't a long-term solution for the group. He was rationing what they were eating, but it wouldn't last forever and they were going through their supplies alarmingly fast.

Whether the smoke cleared soon or not, the time was coming when they would have no choice but to venture out and look for supplies and sustenance. He wondered if there would be anything left out there among the ruins and burned buildings. And what about the looters? Had they cleaned out every available source of food and supplies nearby? Maybe the smoke had affected them, too.

Something was keeping them away, and Vince was surprised that they hadn't returned yet to have another go at his place. He figured they were holed up somewhere, enjoying their ill-gotten spoils. They had probably pillaged enough supplies and alcohol to content themselves for a couple of days.

But that wouldn't last forever, either, and eventually, when they had exhausted all other resources, the looters would come back around. And this time they would be desperate. The list of things Vince and the rest of the survivors needed to do was growing. It was hard to prioritize so many important things they needed to accomplish in order to survive. But somewhere near the top of that list was preparing for another attack and figuring out a way to protect what they had.

Vince knew the key to their success would have to be a good defense. They couldn't rely on firepower alone to defend the garage. Somehow, they needed to stop the looters before they could get close to the garage or even town, for that matter.

They needed a wall of some type—but more than that. There needed to be a way out of the wall: a gate, something that was relatively easy to open and close. After all, Vince and his crew would need to move in and out with their vehicles as well. They couldn't stay within the confines of the town forever. Venturing out would be crucial to their survival.

He mulled over a few ideas in his head but kept coming back to the thing that made the most sense to him: cars. And not just any cars—new cars from the dealership just outside of town. There were hundreds of them parked around the lot at the Chevy dealership, and they should have survived the EMP blast. It seemed as if most cars that had been parked or not running when the bombs hit were still intact. He also noticed that many of them had caught on fire if they were too close to a burning building or house. Fortunately, the car lot was far enough away from the dealership building, so the vehicles in the lot might have survived the intense heat of the fire. At least that was what he hoped.

They would have to take the risk; they needed to get out to the dealership and figure out how to haul the cars back here. Unlike the burned-out wrecks scattered on the roadways, the new cars would be intact, and even though they wouldn't run, they would roll. They could tow them or push them into place and use a couple of large SUVs to make a gate. It was a good-sized dealership, and Vince estimated that there were enough cars to seal off several blocks of town, including the area where his garage and the motel were located.

Of course, in order to make all this happen, they were going to need to clear the roads. They could tow a few cars at a time if they had to, but they wouldn't be able to do that if they had to maneuver around junk all over the road. They needed a piece of equipment large enough to push a car out of their way. The burned-out wrecks wouldn't go easily, either. Vince imagined some might even be fused to the road. After the melting plastic and cheap metal parts had cooled, they would harden in place, making the cars difficult to move.

They needed one of the articulated loaders from the quarry on the other side of the interstate. Vince had no idea if they would run or if they had survived the blast, but they needed to find out.

He'd driven by the quarry countless times but never paid much attention to the equipment. Instead, he spent his time scanning the gravel pits for ducks he'd like to hunt. From what he did remember, though, there were a few older-looking loaders in the yard. At least they looked old; a little rusty and faded from years of sitting out in the sun, they were far from new. With any luck, they were old enough to withstand the effects of the EMPs.

Having one of those big loaders would open up a world of possibilities for them. Not only could they clear roadways, but they could also use the loaders to tow the cars into place and move them around as needed. They could also use the large bucket on the front to move debris around and make sections of their perimeter wall out of what remained of the burned-out buildings around town. In some areas, that would make more sense than using cars.

Of course, this meant they would have to go to the quarry and toward the looters. They had no idea where the gang had gone, but they had come from that direction and escaped the same way. Going to the quarry also meant leaving the motel vulnerable and leaving those who stayed behind to fend for themselves.

The reward outweighed the risk, and even if it didn't, what choice did they have? Getting their hands on the loader was a necessary step in the process of returning to a type of normalcy, not to mention it would ultimately help ensure their safety.

Vince's mind was made up: getting a loader would be their priority. Now he just had to convince the others and figure out who would go and who would stay behind.

. 4 .

Vince slipped a couple of doors down to John's room. He wanted to sell his idea to someone he thought would be honest with him and wouldn't hold back in telling him it was a stupid plan if it truly was. Vince was beginning to believe the others would go along with anything he suggested, and that was far from what he wanted. That was how mistakes were made, and he needed a voice of reason to keep him in check.

Mary would tell him the truth, but when it came to this kind of thing, she would be inclined to go along with whatever he thought. Besides, John had experience, and Vince trusted his opinion.

Vince knocked on John's door but got no answer. He knocked again, a little louder this time, and heard a faint voice from inside.

"Yeah, come in."

Vince opened the door slowly and saw John as he sat up in bed and strained his eyes in the dim yellow light streaming in from outside. Vince was surprised to see John sleeping in the middle of the afternoon. He wanted to chalk it up to the fact that there wasn't much to do, but he suspected it had more to do with John's depression. Not that any of them had it good, but at least they still had their loved ones and families.

"When you get up and get yourself together, why don't you come over to my room so we can talk?" Vince said. "I've got some ideas I want to run by you. I think the smoke has cleared enough to get out of these rooms for a while."

John swung his legs over the side of the bed and sat for a minute, rubbing his hands over his face.

"All right, I'll be over in a minute," he answered.

Vince pulled one of the curtains to the side, letting a little more light into the room before he backed his way out.

"See you in a few, then." Vince closed the door behind him and headed back to his room. On his way, he glanced over at the Ford pickup they had moved to the outer edge of the parking lot last night. He shot a quick wave at Tom, who was taking his turn on watch. Everyone except the kids had stepped up and taken a turn standing a four-hour watch in the truck since their first night in the motel. It was actually a welcome relief from being pent up in the room, and Vince found himself looking forward to his turns.

As he made his way past Cy's room, he knocked on the door.

"Meet me in my room in a couple minutes, okay?" Vince yelled through the door.

"Okay," came Cy's muffled voice from inside the room.

He wanted Cy and John to go with him and try to get the loader; he just hoped John was up for it. He hadn't exactly been himself since he showed up the other night, but who could blame him? The man had lost everything. Vince hated seeing him like this and was worried about his mental health. Being forced to sit around in an old, dim motel room with nothing much to do surely wasn't helping things. They were all a little worse for the wear and suffering from a bad case of cabin fever.

At least the smoke was starting to dissipate and the fires had died down, leaving smoldering piles of rubble. The air was still foul and left a bad taste in your mouth when you went outside, but things were improving slowly. Either that or Vince was getting used to the smell and poor air quality. It was hard to tell, and it had been quite a while since he had seen a patch of blue sky. When the smoke did clear long enough to expose some sky, it was a pale color of yellow that reminded him of the sky sometimes at dusk in a thunderstorm, only more of an unnatural shade.

He couldn't help but wonder if it was a direct

result of the nukes or a byproduct of the fires. He hoped it was the latter and that the sky would return to normal after the atmosphere cleared. They could desperately use some rain to put out the rest of the fires and wash the ash off everything, but he wasn't hopeful.

When he entered the room, Mary was throwing an empty water bottle for Nugget, who was thankful for the attention and no doubt feeling the effects of being confined to the room for far too long like the rest of them.

"It looks a little better out there than it did yesterday at this time." Vince tried to hide his disappointment in the conditions outside. He had hoped for more of an improvement over yesterday.

"I was just looking out the window, thinking maybe I could take Nugget out for a walk around," she replied. Nugget's ears perked up at the sound of her name, and she twisted her head. There was a knock at the door, and then it opened. Cy stood at the door for a second before coming into the room.

"What's up?" he asked.

"That was quick," Vince said.

He smirked. "Yeah, well, there's only so much solitaire a guy can play."

Vince hadn't told Mary about his plan yet, either. They had discussed the fact that they needed to secure the garage and motel in some way, but Vince had kept the details to himself.

"I want to get a team together and go over to the quarry to see if we can get one of those loaders running." Vince wanted to wait for John to join them so there would be another experienced voice of reason in the room, but he couldn't hold it in anymore.

"Let's do it. I'm game," Cy blurted out.

Vince knew Cy would be on board; he never doubted that. He would have done anything to escape the boredom of the motel room for a while and find a change of scenery. But Mary didn't respond right away, and Vince could tell she was thinking about what he had said.

"Do you think it's safe to go over there? That's the way the looters went. And what about the smoke? Is it safe to be outside for that long?"

"Well, the air's not great, but I think we need to act soon, before they come back. We need the loader to clear the roads and help build a wall."

"A wall?" John walked into the room and joined the conversation. He still looked the worse for wear, and although they'd had plenty of time to rest, he still looked like he could use some sleep.

"My dad wants to try and grab a loader from the quarry," Cy said.

John paused for a moment and rubbed his chin. "That's not a bad idea," he said.

"It would make clearing the roads a lot easier, and I thought maybe we could use it to make a perimeter around some of the town," Vince explained. "We could use the cars from the dealership for the front part of the barricade facing the interstate and a couple big SUVs for a gate. We'll figure out what areas we want to be inside the barricade as we make our way around town. I'm thinking at least a few blocks south into town."

"And we can use the material we clear off the roads to build the wall in the areas that we want to be more permanent," John added.

"It won't stop anyone from getting in if they want to," Vince started, "but it will stop them from entering town in vehicles and force them to be on foot. They'll be easier to deal with that way. We'll keep a person on watch and we'll have a defendable position." Vince looked at Mary. She seemed to be the only one with doubt in her eyes.

"I'm just worried you'll run into trouble out there," she said. "They killed Jim, remember?"

Vince nodded. "I do. But that's all the more reason to try and keep them out."

· 5 ·

It took a little more convincing to get Mary on board, but ultimately, she gave in and agreed that it was a good idea. Vince hadn't expected her to give him such a hard time about his plan and was quickly reminded that she was someone who would speak her mind, especially when it came to their safety.

Once they had worked out the details and organized their thoughts, they gathered the others and laid out the plan to ask for their input. Everyone was on board with the idea, and Tom volunteered to join Vince, John, and Cy. Vince was glad they were all in agreement, although if he was being honest with himself, he had already made up his mind, regardless of what the others thought.

Tom was familiar with the family who owned the quarry, and as far as he knew, they hadn't survived the attack. They lived a couple of blocks away from Tom's house, and he remembered it being lost to the fire when he and his family were forced to flee their neighborhood.

This gave Vince and the others a clear conscience about commandeering the loader. Taking the equipment was certainly something that weighed on his mind and almost discouraged him from following through with the plan in the beginning. In his mind, it was basically stealing, and he wondered if that made him just as bad as the looters. It was for the greater good, but that didn't make him feel any better about taking something that wasn't his.

Of course, these were unusual circumstances. After all, they were prepared to take advantage of the motel, and he hadn't given that a second thought. He eventually settled on the notion that when it came to procuring supplies and whatever else they needed to survive, there would be a lot of gray areas in the days and weeks to come. As much as he hated the sound of it, that was just the way things were now.

Fred would stand watch and keep an eye on things at the motel while they went to get the loader. After witnessing Jim's death, Bill was still a little off in Vince's opinion, and he was thankful that the others were keeping it together so well.

In particular, he was impressed with Reese. She wasn't what he had expected from a girl her age, and she seemed to be adapting well to the tough conditions and circumstances they were being forced to deal with. Among the dreary faces of the others over the last few days, she was a welcome bright spot. She always had an encouraging word or two for anyone who cared to talk and managed to even smile on occasion. She reminded Vince that there was a future for them in this bleak world, and he was thankful to have her in the group of survivors.

Vince and his small team could keep in touch with the others thanks to John. John had a couple of handheld radios with him, along with the other supplies he had in his Bronco. Fortunately, he was able to clean out his patrol car before it went up in flames. To their arsenal he added his .45-caliber Glock G21 service pistol, a Colt AR-15 chambered in .223, and another 12-gauge Remington shotgun. He had a decent amount of ammo for all of the guns he brought with him, and Vince was beginning to feel better about their situation and their ability to defend themselves.

As grateful as Vince was to have the additional weapons, he was most thankful for the two-way radios. He would have liked to have a couple more, but it was better than having no communication at all. If something happened in town while Vince and his team were away, they could at least be notified and head back as quickly as they could to help. And if they needed backup, the others were there for them as well, although Vince would need a good reason to call for help and take them away from the relative safety of the motel.

Vince glanced at his watch and noted that it was almost 6:00 p.m. With the waning sunlight struggling to break through the still-thick air, it seemed much later than that. Darkness would come early, like it had the past few nights, thanks to the dark gray cloud of smoke that hung ominously over the town. They needed to leave soon if they were going to make it back before nightfall, although it might already be too late for that.

The roads were tough enough to navigate during the daylight hours. With any luck, one of them would be driving the loader back, and it might or might not have working lights. Vince had never driven a piece of equipment that large before, and neither had any of the others. He was confident one of them would figure it out, but the articulated steering would be tricky to get used to and might make it tough to navigate on a road littered with obstacles.

On top of all that, they had to hotwire the loader. He figured that would fall on his and Cy's shoulders, and he was glad Cy would be with him to help figure it out. If they couldn't find the key, they would have to hotwire the thing, and that might take a little time to work out. Vince had never hotwired a car before, but he understood the basic concept. Still, there were no guarantees that a commercial loader would have wiring that even resembled that of a passenger car.

He planned on grabbing an assortment of tools from the garage. Then it would be up to him and Cy to figure it out together when they got there. Add in the very real possibility of having another run-in with the looters and the odds quickly began to stack up against them. Hotwiring the loader would be a challenge, but doing so under gunfire would be something entirely different.

With any luck, they'd be able to slip in and grab the loader unnoticed. The quarry was only about six or seven miles past the interstate on the other side of town. Funny how it never seemed as far away as it did right now.

They decided to take Jim's Jeep. The old CJ-7 had a soft top that could be put down, giving them a clear shot out of the vehicle in almost any direction. Vince hoped it wouldn't come to that, but if it did, shooting from the open Jeep would be easier than shooting from a closed-in vehicle. Of course, they would also be more exposed, but it was a risk they were going to have to take.

They loaded up and headed over to his garage so Vince could grab a few tools. He ran inside and gathered a hammer, pliers, a few screwdrivers, wire-strippers, and some electrical tape. He'd never attempted to hotwire a vehicle, so he paused for a moment to have a look around the garage. He wasn't sure what else to take and decided to go with what he had. Maybe he'd catch a break, find the key to the loader, and wouldn't need any of these things. He threw the tools in a bag and hurried back to the others in the Jeep outside.

"All set?" John asked from the driver's seat.

"I think so." Vince threw the bag of tools on the floor by his feet and looked back at Cy, who was sitting in the back with Tom. Both Cy and Tom carried AR-15s. John had his Glock holstered on his hip and the 12-gauge stuffed between his seat and the center console. Vince was only carrying his .45, figuring he'd have his hands full with the tools and hopefully operating the loader.

Vince squeezed the button on the handheld radio with his thumb. "Come in, Fred. Do you copy? Over."

"Roger that," Fred replied. "Loud and clear."

Vince was glad to hear Fred using proper radio protocol. He had stressed how important it was to communicate correctly with the radios and hoped Fred didn't think he was being too picky. But he knew that in a high-stress situation, following proper procedure was important to ensure that the lines stayed clear of any unnecessary chatter. It was also important to end with the message "over" so that the other person knew when it was clear to speak and both sides weren't trying to talk over each other. In Vince's mind, there was hardly anything more annoying than someone who was button-happy on the radio.

As they pulled out of the garage parking lot and drove toward the quarry, Vince waved to Fred, who acknowledged him from his watch position in the Ford pickup at the edge of the motel parking lot. They quickly lost sight of him and the motel as they headed out of town and navigated their way through the wrecks and burned-out vehicles that littered the road.

John slowly picked up speed as they approached the interstate overpass. Vince glanced back at his son, but Cy was preoccupied with the scenery and keeping a lookout for the looters, like they had discussed. Vince was proud of the boy and stopped mid-thought to remind himself that he was no longer a boy. Cy was a man now and had been for some time. The world they now faced would wash away what little innocence remained of his youth.

Vince focused on the road ahead and helped John navigate. He hoped they weren't attempting this too soon and began to second-guess the plan as they lost sight of town altogether. Reminding himself that they really had no choice was of little consolation.

· 6 ·

As they approached the underpass that led to the other side of I-70, they drove by what remained of a burned-out McDonald's on the right-hand side of the road and a still-smoldering pile of rubble that had been the Royal Travel Plaza. No one said anything as they gawked at what was left of the familiar landmarks that once greeted people entering Cloverdale from the busy interstate.

The quarry was only a few miles north of town, and the property itself started just after the exit ramps to I-70 on the left-hand side of the road. Vince didn't know for sure how big it was, but he guessed it had to be a few thousand acres, including the large blue water-filled quarry pits that lay at the closest point along the road.

Unfortunately, the quarry entrance was located on the north side of the property and would require them to continue for a few more miles before they reached 800 South and made the left that would lead them to the gravel yard.

That was where Vince had seen the equipment parked the last time he was out this way. A new section of the quarry had recently been opened, and the workers had just started digging the new pit only a few months ago. Vince was glad the loader was closer to the front of the property and that they wouldn't have to go too far into the yard to reach it, but a part of him wished it wasn't so close to the road.

The plan was simple, really: Vince and Cy would try to start one of the loaders while John and Fred kept an eye out. They'd check out the quarry office first to see if it was still standing and to look for the keys, but based on what Vince had seen, he wasn't holding out much hope of the building still being there.

John slowed down as they approached 800 South, and he was forced to cut across the corner of the intersection in order to avoid what was left of an eighteen-wheeler. Its early-morning gravel run unexpectedly interrupted by the EMPs, the truck blocked the small two-lane road leading to the quarry and had long since burned down to the frame. Its fiberglass and plastic sleeper cab was barely recognizable. Melted and still smoking, the truck's plastic parts had run down the frame and poured across the blacktop like a cooling lava flow.

Vince wondered if the driver had escaped or been reduced to ashes and was now part of the melted mess.

These were the types of things Vince was worried about. How many trucks and other vehicles had fused themselves to the road due to the intense heat of the unchecked fires. As they passed the truck and drove back on the road, he wondered if the loader would even have enough power to clear a mess like that. It looked pretty permanent to him, and wrecks like this wouldn't get any easier to push off the road as things cooled and solidified in place.

John made the next left into the quarry entrance and slowed down as the Jeep bounced over the rough gravel road that led past the main office. The chain-link gate was wide open, and Vince was thankful for that as he realized he probably should have brought a pair of bolt-cutters with him.

"I guess there's no point in looking for keys," John said. The quarry office was no longer there; in its place was a pile of charred and smoking debris. It was no surprise, and Vince had expected as much. Nobody paid much attention to it as they drove past and headed deeper into the quarry.

The road narrowed as they passed a section bordered by an abandoned gravel pit filled with dark blue water to their left and towering piles of aggregate to their right. Vince felt uneasy, knowing that this was the only way in and out of the quarry. It was a definite choke point if someone wanted to block their exit. If the looters came after them, they could easily close the road off, leaving them no choice but to fight their way out.

Vince looked around nervously in every direction but didn't see anything he considered suspicions. Although he tried to calm his nerves, he couldn't deny the feeling that they were being watched. He tried to convince himself he was just being paranoid. It didn't help put his mind at ease, and he couldn't shake it. The narrow road and the fact that the sky was darkening by the minute wasn't helping.

"What's wrong?" Cy asked.

"Nothing. Just keep your eyes peeled." Vince didn't want to let on how bothered he was, but he suspected that John felt the same by the way he was scanning their surroundings. The expression on John's face was tense and he hadn't said a word since they passed the burned-down office.

Vince looked at John. "What do you think?"

"I don't like it," John answered. "This is the only way in or out of here."

Tom leaned forward between the seats, biting his lip. "You think we should go back? Maybe we should go back."

"No, we're here. Let's do what we came to do and get out of here as soon as we can," Vince said.

"Agreed." John nodded and sped up. The road took a sharp right turn and then spilled into a wide-open yard with heavy equipment on the far side. There were a handful of machines in the yard, but an old John Deer 544B caught Vince's eye. He wasn't very familiar with heavy equipment outside of tractors, but he recognized that it was an older loader by the body styling and the dull yellow paint that was half flaked off the rusty exterior.

Vince pointed. "Let's try that one over there." He and Cy gathered the tools and their weapons as John headed toward the old loader. He swung the Jeep around in a wide turn and slid to a stop in the loose gravel.

"I'll head back out toward the entrance and wait there," John said.

"Don't go too far," Vince said, glancing at the cab of the enclosed loader. "I'm not even sure we can get this thing started. Plus, you'll have to give one of us a ride back. There's only room for one in there."

"We'll wait up there, where the yard opens up after the curve. We won't let you out of our sight." John nodded as Cy climbed over the back seat and jumped out of the open Jeep. He joined his dad as John began to pull away and head toward the entrance.

Tools and guns in hand, Vince and Cy started over to the loader. Vince glanced back at the dimming taillights on the Jeep and suddenly felt very alone. The crunch of gravel under their feet was the only sound, and an eerie silence fell over them. He continued to watch as the Jeep almost disappeared halfway around the sharp turn and into the yard before the brake lights lit up and it stopped. He was hoping John would stay a little closer to them, but he probably figured their biggest threat would come from the road. It was the smart thing to do, and Vince tried to put the uneasiness out of his mind and focus his attention on the loader.

Cy was already halfway up the metal stair treads that led to the cab of the loader by the time his dad joined him near the equipment. He had wanted to take the lead on this and prove himself to his father.

He often wondered if his dad really respected him as a mechanic, mostly due to the fact that he worked on bikes for a living. They teased each other on occasion, but he couldn't help but think some of the jokes his dad made about him working on motorcycles were genuine.

If he could figure out how to start this loader on his own, it would put an end to any doubts his dad had about his abilities. And Cy had good reason to believe he could do it. After all, he had an ace up his sleeve. This wasn't the first time he had attempted to hotwire a piece of construction equipment.

When Cy was in high school, he used to hang out with a group of friends who rode dirt bikes on the weekends and any chance they could get. One of those friends lived in a new housing development on the outskirts of town. The area was a dirt biker's dream. The unfinished roads and empty acreage provided miles of riding fun. But being the rowdy teens that they were, it wasn't enough to keep them out of trouble.

On one Saturday night in particular, one of his friends proposed the idea of using the developer's dirt-moving equipment to build some jumps. Of course, this required hotwiring one of the loaders on site and a lack of better judgment on Cy's part. He was the one to figure out how to start the thing and, unfortunately, the one who got caught driving it when the cops showed up. It turned out that driving a large, yellow, brightly lit machine around in the middle of the night wasn't something the residents of the development were willing to ignore.

It was the dumbest thing he'd ever been a part of and he regretted it to this day. Fortunately, his mother knew the developer and was able to smooth things over for him and his friends. No charges were filed, and she agreed not to tell his father about the incident, something he was very thankful for, although he wasn't sure if keeping the secret was for his sake or hers.

None of that mattered anymore and seemed like it was a lifetime ago. He briefly thought about sharing the story with his dad but decided not to right now. Instead, he chose to concentrate on the task at hand. There would be time for that later, and it would probably go over better if he was successful.

As he searched for a key in the obvious places, the reality of the situation set in. It wasn't going to be that easy. Not that he had any illusions about what they were doing, but he hadn't ruled out finding a key tucked away under a visor or the seat. That only happened in the movies anyway, right?

"Any luck finding a key?" Vince asked.

Cy looked down at his dad on the ground below. "Nothing."

"Want me to take a look?" Vince started up the metal treads.

"I got it." Cy backed out of the cab, partway blocking Vince's ascent, and got under the console near the ignition. "Maybe hold a light for me." He expected an argument from his dad but was surprised when Vince simply turned his flashlight in his direction and remained silent.

The pressure was on. Not only was everyone counting on them to bring back the loader, but now he had to prove to his dad that he could rise to the challenge and get this done. On top of that, he couldn't help but wonder if they would have a run-in with the looters again while they were out.

. 7 .

Cy struggled to make sense of the rat's nest of multicolored wires under the console as the inadequate light from his dad's flashlight dimly lit the cab of the loader. All he needed to do was isolate the wires coming off the ignition, but the years of quarry dust had caked onto them, making it difficult to distinguish what was what. The fact that he had contorted himself into a very uncomfortable position in order to see under the console wasn't helping matters, either.

"Can you hand me the wire-strippers?" Cy asked. He heard his dad rummaging through the bag of tools before he felt the rubber handle make contact with his outstretched hand.

"There you go. What do you think?" Vince strained to see what Cy was doing.

"I think I need to knock some of this dirt off of the wires so I can see what I'm doing under here."

Cy used the tool as a small club and clumsily

smacked the cluster of wires a few times. Without room to pull his head out from under the console, he closed his eyes and grimaced as fine gravel dust fell from the wires and coated his face.

"Oh, man. That was nice." Cy spit out some of the dirt that had landed in his mouth and felt the grit crunch between his teeth. But it was a small price to pay for making out the color-coded wires that ran out of the ignition switch.

He spit out another mixture of saliva and dirt as he carefully picked out the ignition wire and the starter wire from the cluster. Using the blunt jaws of the wire-stripper, he firmly gripped the first wire and slowly but forcefully pulled it out of the ignition switch. Then he did the same for the second wire.

Next, he stripped the ends of both wires until he had about an inch or so of exposed frayed wire at the ends. Then he twisted those together individually until they were neat and tight spirals. This was it—the moment of truth.

"Well, here goes nothing."

"You better make sure it's…" But before Vince could get the words out, Cy touched the two bare ends together and was rewarded with a spark followed by a loud cough from the engine. The large machine lurched from its position and threw Cy into the console, where he hit his head against the unforgiving steel frame of the cab.

"Whoa!" Vince hung on to the cab door and nearly lost his footing as the loader jumped forward a couple of feet. The sudden movement startled Cy enough that he let go of the wires and broke the connection, causing the engine to stall out and the loader to jerk backward this time. It threw him in the opposite direction and drove his shoulder into the base of the seat mount with a solid *thunk*.

"I was just about to say 'make sure it's in neutral before you try to start it,' but I guess we know it isn't now." Vince sighed as he readjusted himself on the steps.

"At least we know it runs." Cy rubbed his head and felt a small knot welling up.

"You okay?" Vince asked.

"Yeah, I'm fine." And he was, physically; it was his pride that hurt the most. Cy looked down at the gear selection lever on the column and saw that the indicator was halfway between neutral and low gear. He must have bumped it while he was trying to position himself under the console. He shifted the lever into neutral and wiggled it a little to make sure it was secure before he turned his attention back to the wires.

Vince hopped off the bottom step and landed on the gravel. "I think I'll watch from down here this time."

"I don't blame you." Cy smiled and was glad to see his dad taking his mistake so lightly. Reaching under the ignition as he sat down behind the wheel, he felt the two dangling wires and pulled them out from under the console so he could see them. He held them with one hand and then used the other to quickly twist the two ends together. Once more a small spark flashed and the engine roared to life.

Cy looked back through the rear cab window and saw a large puff of black smoke jump from the exhaust pipe as the engine revved up and then slowed to a smooth idle. For as rough as the old loader looked, he was impressed by how well it was running.

His dad climbed back up to the cab and tossed the bag of tools on the floor, then handed Cy his AR-15.

"Sounds pretty good. You okay to drive this thing, or do you want me to run it back to town?" Vince asked.

"I'm good. I got it." Cy was already putting the bucket through its positions and familiarizing himself with the controls for the hydraulics. He glanced at his dad, who was still half in the cab and looking at him.

"Seriously, Dad, I can handle it. No problem."

Vince nodded. "I know you can." He started to climb down and then paused.

"How about giving me a ride over to the Jeep?" Vince asked.

Cy shrugged. "Sure, but there's not much room in here."

"No problem. I'll ride in the bucket." Vince jumped down to the ground, then looked up at Cy and shot him a crooked smile. "Go slow."

Cy nodded as he pulled the cab door closed. He raised the bucket a couple of feet off the ground and leveled it off so his dad could easily climb in and sit down comfortably. It was much quieter with the door closed, and the seat was surprisingly comfortable. The feeling of power that washed over him as he sat there behind the wheel of the large loader was intoxicating, and for a brief moment, he forgot about what was going on around them.

Once his dad was situated in the bucket and had given a thumbs-up, Cy pushed down on the brake and put the loader into the L position, which he assumed meant low. There was also an H on the column for what he also guessed was high gear. Until he was confident and got used to the handling, he'd keep it in low, especially with his dad riding in the bucket.

As he eased his foot off the brake and onto the gas pedal, the big machine began to roll forward. He cut the wheel and headed for the taillights of the Jeep on the other side of the gravel yard. Slowly but surely, they made their way to John and Tom, who were waiting and watching. Both smiled when Cy pulled up alongside the Jeep.

As soon as he stopped, his dad climbed out of the bucket and headed back toward the loader's cab. Cy cracked the door open as his dad approached.

"You still want to drive it back?" Vince asked.

Cy nodded. "Yeah, no problem."

"All right then. You lead the way and we'll follow you home." Vince paused as he began to turn around and head to the Jeep.

"How's your fuel?"

"I'm good. Almost a full tank," Cy answered. Vince nodded and continued to the Jeep. Cy gave the guys a small wave as he passed them and started down the gravel road to the quarry's exit. As he rumbled and bounced along, he felt invincible sitting up high in the fully enclosed cab of the loader.

He glanced back at the headlights of the Jeep and turned the wheel unintentionally as he strained to look behind him. The loader swerved sharply to the left and he overcompensated by turning the wheel the other way in an effort to correct it, but this only made it worse and caused the loader to swerve and bounce. The articulated body on the loader was something he would have to get used to; it would be easy to lose control if he didn't pay attention to what he was doing.

Once he straightened the loader out, he resolved to concentrate and worry less about his dad and the others behind him. He hoped his dad hadn't noticed his mistake, but he knew better. How could they miss the big yellow loader wildly swerving back and forth in front of them? He promised himself he wouldn't let that happen again and gripped the wheel a little tighter.

He slowed down at the end of the gravel road and only glanced at the burned ruins of the quarry office as he passed. When he reached the edge of the paved road, he mashed the brake pedal down, and the loader came to a stop with a low moan. Cy made a mental note about the soft brakes and checked both directions for traffic. The last thing he wanted to do was run into something or someone because he couldn't stop in time. He felt a little foolish checking for traffic before he pulled out since he knew there was nobody on the roads and there was no traffic to look out for. Or was there?

· 8 ·

It took a moment to sink in, but when it finally did, the realization that there were headlights coming toward them sent a cold chill down Cy's spine. If he had to guess, the lights were a mile or two in the distance, but there was no mistaking the smaller lights as those of an ATV. The brighter set of headlights had to belong to a car or truck.

Cy froze and stared in disbelief for a second, trying to rationalize that maybe the others from the motel had come to help them with the loader, but he knew it was the looters.

He glanced back at the Jeep as it closed in on his position. Then it hit him that he should turn the lights off on the loader. He hit the switch and he was instantly enveloped in the darkness. He popped open the cab door and stepped out carefully, trying to keep his balance while he waved at his dad and the others.

A section of tall bushes and weeds lined the gravel road near the entrance to the quarry, and Cy knew that his dad wouldn't be able to see the approaching headlights from his lower position in the Jeep. Thankfully, from his elevated position in the loader, Cy spotted the looters over the vegetation.

With any luck, the looters hadn't seen his lights, although he doubted it. The four large floodlights adorning the upper part of the cab and the two others sitting at the top of the hydraulic arms that operated the bucket were extremely bright. The lights easily lit up a good fifty yards or so of road in front of the loader. It'd be a miracle if he hadn't been spotted in the surrounding darkness.

He waved frantically at John as the Jeep pulled up next to the loader and motioned for him to kill the lights. John finally figured out what Cy was trying to tell him and turned them off as the Jeep came to an abrupt stop.

"The looters, they're back. Over that way." Cy pointed east, toward the road that led back to the interstate and Cloverdale. He was surprised, and a little relieved, to see the lights still so far away. Maybe they hadn't been spotted after all.

Vince and John hurried out of the Jeep and climbed up the loader, where they joined Cy outside the cab to get a better look down the road.

"That's them, all right. No doubt about it," Vince said.

John produced a pair of small binoculars and glassed the approaching vehicles. "Can't see much. Still a lot of smoke in the air. Definitely at least one car and a few four-wheelers. Not really sure how many people there are. Here, have a look." John handed the binoculars to Vince.

Vince let out a frustrated grunt. "I'm pretty sure that's the same car I unloaded on at the gas station. I guess they got it patched up."

"Do you think they saw us?" Cy asked.

"Hard to say," John said. "They're not moving very fast, but that could be because of the visibility."

"Or maybe the double-aught buckshot in the radiator," Vince added with a smirk.

"Hey, guys, what's going on?" Tom shouted nervously from the Jeep. He was standing up in the back seat and hanging on to the roll bar.

"Looters, but we're not sure where they're headed," John answered.

"What are we gonna do?" Cy asked.

"We need to wait and see which way they're headed," John said. "They haven't reached the intersection yet, and if they don't come this way, there's no reason to engage them in a fight, at least not right now." He glanced at Vince.

Vince nodded. "I agree."

"And what if they're headed back to my dad's garage or the motel to finish what they started?" Cy bit his lip and looked at John, then at his dad.

"Well, we obviously can't let them do that," Vince responded. The three watched impatiently from the top of the loader as the looters continued to head toward the intersection where the burned eighteen-wheeler blocked the road.

In the best-case scenario, they would turn and head north, away from the quarry and Cloverdale, but Cy didn't believe for one second that they would do that. He knew in his gut that they were coming back for the supplies at his dad's garage or, even worse, revenge. He was pretty sure his dad and John knew that, too. He also hoped they had a plan to deal with them.

They continued to watch from the loader as the headlights weaved and threaded their way around unseen obstacles. They seemed to be traveling in a single-file line and looked more organized than the last time they haphazardly drove into town. Cy could hear the louder ATVs now, and the fact that they were going to have to deal with these people one way or another once again became very real.

Cy could see them clearly enough now to count four ATVs and two cars. One of the cars was missing a headlight, and he had mistaken it for an ATV when he first spotted the group approaching. The cars were leading the entourage, with the ATV's taking up the rear of the column.

"There's another car," Cy said.

"I see that," John replied.

Then it happened: the cars turned and the ATVs followed close behind. They were heading south toward Cloverdale. It was a bittersweet moment; the looters hadn't spotted the bright lights of the loader, but they were definitely headed back to his dad's garage and to undoubtedly exact revenge on the survivors.

· 9 ·

"We need to let the others know," Vince said. He regretted not getting in touch with Fred on the radio sooner. He was sure the looters had seen the bright spotlights on the loader and would head their way. He should have contacted Fred as soon as they saw them.

"Tom, get Fred on the radio. Let him know to get the others ready. The looters are headed back to town."

Vince climbed down, skipping the last step and jumping to the ground. He ignored the pain in his back and made his way over to the Jeep while Tom attempted to contact Fred on the two-way.

Tom was shaking his head and handed the radio to Vince as soon as he reached the Jeep. "Nothing," he said, shrugging. "it's not going through, Major."

Vince tried. "Fred, do you copy? Come in. Over." But there was no answer. Vince tried a couple more times but heard no response.

John had joined him at the Jeep and was climbing into the driver's seat.

"We need to get going. We're wasting time here. We can't let the looters catch them off guard." He started the Jeep.

Vince stood there, conflicted and unable to make a decision; he looked back at Cy, who was still on top of the loader and looking to him for direction. Suddenly, this plan of his seemed like a very bad idea. The others needed them now, but he didn't want to leave his son here by himself.

"Just go! I'll be right behind you," Cy shouted as he climbed back into the cab of the loader and began closing the door. Vince had no choice in the matter, and he knew it. They had to move if they were going to catch the looters. Cy would have to bring up the rear on his own.

Vince thought about abandoning the plan for the time being and telling Cy to come with them in the Jeep, but then all this would be for nothing, and besides, they really needed that loader. Now that they had done the work and hotwired the thing, it would be easy pickings for the looters if they decided to take it for themselves.

Vince reluctantly climbed into the Jeep, and before he could say anything to Cy, the rear wheels began to spin in the gravel as John put his foot down and made the turn out onto the paved road. Vince looked back and saw the loader lights ignite through a cloud of dust left behind by John's quick departure.

There were so many thoughts racing through Vince's mind right now, but there was no time to make sense of any of them. They had to catch the looters before they reached the motel. With the radio not working, the others would be completely caught off guard and an attack would certainly produce casualties.

Vince was troubled and briefly overcome with a sense of remorse for leaving them so vulnerable and unprepared. In hindsight, he should have planned better. He wasn't sure how or what else he could have done, but that didn't rid him of the gut-wrenching guilt he felt at the moment.

John held out for as long as he could and managed to make it to the main road leading back to town before he flicked on the Jeep's headlights. Vince was surprised that he waited for as long as he had, considering the speed they were traveling and the poor visibility. He was glad John was driving. Vince's nerves would have given out long ago and he would have turned the lights on much sooner.

Tom leaned forward, between the front seats. "What are we going to do?"

"I'm not sure, but we can't let them get into town." John glanced back at Tom. "Just get ready and don't hesitate to use your weapon."

Tom leaned back into his seat and brought the AR-15 up to his lap. Vince heard the familiar sound of the charging handle as Tom chambered a round and readied himself. Vince grabbed the 12-gauge wedged between the console and the seat and followed suit by pumping a shell into the action of the gun. It was a better choice than his .45, especially if he was going to be shooting from the Jeep at moving targets.

Luckily for them, the ATVs were at the rear of the pack, and with any luck, the riders wouldn't notice or hear the Jeep approaching over the loud exhaust note of their four-wheelers. The riders were all wearing helmets this time as well, another advantage for Vince and the others. The helmets would restrict the looters' vision and hopefully prevent them from seeing the Jeep as it came up from behind—at least until Vince and the others were close enough to take action.

Vince glanced back, trying his best to locate the loader. He didn't see Cy anywhere, and the possibility of the loader breaking down or stalling crossed his mind.

Vince wasn't sure how fast the old machine would go, but he doubted Cy could coax much more than twenty or thirty miles per hour out of it, even in high gear. The old John Deere wasn't made for speed and it was well past its prime.

It sounded solid when they started it up, but

there could be a big difference in how it idled and how it would tolerate being run flat-out. He knew his son and was certain that Cy would push the loader to its limits in hopes of catching up with them. Hopefully, the dated machine would run better than it looked. The last thing he wanted to think about was Cy ending up stranded. If that happened, Vince would have to go back for him.

And what if there were more looters on their way? If he broke down, Cy would be a sitting duck on the side of the road. He had his AR-15 with him, but the all-glass cab of the loader wouldn't provide much cover and it would leave him very exposed in the event of an attack. This was all the more reason for Vince to take out the looters in front of him as quickly as possible and return to his son.

He readjusted himself in the seat as he turned his attention to the taillights of the ATVs. They were not that far ahead anymore. The riders on the ATVs had spaced themselves out more than when they had first attacked the garage, and there was about a fifty-yard gap between them as they drove in a semi-straight line.

John killed the lights again as they closed in on the last ATV in the column.

"We might be able to get close before they notice us without the lights. I can follow their taillights from here," John shouted without taking his eyes off the road or his hands off the wheel.

Vince glanced over at the speedometer and saw that they were only going fifty miles per hour. With the top down on the Jeep and the wind rushing by, it felt like they were doing twice that. Or maybe the adrenaline pumping through his veins had made it feel like they were rolling down the highway at a much higher speed.

Now, less than twenty yards away from the closest ATV, Vince could see a single rider bent over the handlebars, shotgun slung over his shoulder.

"Take your time and make your shots count," John cautioned. Vince readied the shotgun and prepared himself to do what was necessary. It wasn't easy for him, and he felt conflicted about whether to aim for the ATV or the man driving.

The answer was clear, but he was reluctant to accept it. Even if Vince shot the tire out or something, the driver would likely die in the crash. And if he didn't and was only hurt, he would become a liability with a loaded gun. If he didn't shoot at the Jeep, he would be there for Cy to deal with when he came along.

This was no game, and the looters had established the stakes when they shot and killed Jim at the motel and continued to fire on him and Bill. The time for thinking was over—it was time for action.

· 10 ·

John sped up gradually as he closed the last couple of yards between the Jeep and the ATV. Before Vince knew it, they were nearly side by side with the four-wheeler. The rider noticed the Jeep at the last second and turned his head, but it was too late.

Vince saw the terrified expression on the rider's face as he pulled the trigger and flames leaped from the end of the barrel. He hit him squarely in the chest, exactly as Vince intended. He didn't want to take any chances and have the shot deflected by the helmet, although at that short distance, it probably wouldn't have mattered.

The rider was blown sideways off the ATV, and the limp body rolled along the shoulder of the road before coming to a stop in the grass. The ATV swerved left, into the front fender of the Jeep, and ricocheted off in the opposite direction until it turned sideways and they passed it.

Vince watched in the sideview mirror as the ATV flipped violently several times until it finally landed upside down and slid off the road in a shower of sparks. For a second, the man's face flashed through Vince's mind. Then he shook away the thought and turned his full attention to the next looter in line.

John nodded. "Good job! Looks like nobody noticed, either."

Vince found that hard to believe as his ears still rung from the blast of the shotgun. Even with the Jeep's top down, the report of the gun had echoed off the front windshield and left him reeling a little from the shockwave. He made a mental note to lean out past the body of the vehicle next time he took a shot.

Tom must have noticed he was a little rattled; he leaned up and put his hand on Vince's shoulder. "I got the next one. Hold her steady, John."

With that, Tom began to make his way to his feet. Carefully hanging on to the roll bar, he slowly pulled himself up and into position while he braced against the wind. With one arm wrapped under the roll bar, he hung on while he used the other arm to move the AR-15 into position. Standing with both feet firmly planted on the back seat, he steadied himself and lined up the shot on the next ATV.

"A little closer," he said, half out loud. "Just a little bit more... Steady."

Vince watched as they gained on the next looter in line and was caught off guard by the sharp crack of the AR. A bright yellow flash of light cut through the darkness inside the Jeep as Vince kept his eyes trained on the target. But nothing happened—at least not at first. Then the rider turned his head and glanced back in their direction. The shot had missed, and they had been spotted!

The driver began to flash the ATV's lights at the others in front of him and took evasive maneuvers by swerving back and forth. The rider seemed confused and panicked; he stopped swerving and slowed down as he attempted to break right, toward the shoulder of the road, with a sharp turn.

"Again!" John barked. Not more than a few seconds passed before another sharp crack rang out, accompanied by a hot yellow muzzle flash from the AR. The rider didn't turn around this time or seem to pay the shot any mind. Vince thought it was another miss and prepared to ready his shotgun when the rider suddenly slumped over the handlebars. The ATV slowed and veered off the road, where it continued rolling for several yards until it came to rest in the taller grass. The rider remained hunched over the gas tank as they passed by.

Tom had succeeded in taking out another in the group, but not before the remaining invaders had seen the flashing lights of their now-dead gang member. The remaining two ATVs peeled off to the left and right while the lead car sped up. The second car in line, the black sedan Vince had shot up at the garage, slowed down a little and broke to the left. Eventfully, the black car made its way over to the grassy median and began to double back around them as it threw up large rooster tails of grass and dirt.

Vince had lost track of the ATVs at this point, something that made him very nervous. He looked at John, who was already applying pressure to the brakes and preparing to turn.

"Hold on!" he yelled as he cut the wheel. Vince glanced back to check on Tom, who was, last he'd seen, standing up on the rear seat and hanging on to the roll bar. But Tom had already come down from his shooting position and was clutching his gun.

"Now what!" Tom grimaced as he held on to the seat and tried to keep from sliding to one side.

"We have to let the others know," Vince shouted as the force of the turn pressed him against the door. "The lead car is still headed for town."

John grunted as he continued through the turn behind the black sedan. "I don't have any choice. I have to follow this guy and the four-wheelers or they'll come up behind us and take us out."

As they made the turn and approached the other side of the road, Vince spotted a burned-out wreck not too far away. It was the remains of a small passenger car, but it looked intact enough to provide him cover.

"Drop me off, John."

"What? Where?" John stammered.

"Right here. I'll hide behind that car and you can bring them back by here. I'll ambush them if you bring 'em by close enough."

"You sure you want to do this?" John looked at Vince as he slowed the Jeep down even more.

"What choice do we have? We need to split up anyway. Tom can stay with you and keep them busy with the AR. I'll take the radio with me and try to warn the others about the first car."

Before John had a chance to argue, Vince had the door open and his leg halfway through, waiting for John to slow down enough for him to bail out.

John slammed on the brakes and Vince hopped out.

"Go, go!" Vince slammed the door shut and headed for the wreck.

"Be careful, Major." Tom's words trailed off as the Jeep peeled out in the grass and continued the chase. Vince hoped that between the darkness and the dust the vehicles had kicked up while cutting through the median, the looters wouldn't notice his exit from the jeep.

He sprinted the ten or fifteen yards to what was left of the burned-out car sitting in the far-right lane of the northbound side of the highway. Clutching the radio in one hand and the shotgun in the other, he took a position on the far side of the wreck and crouched down to catch his breath. He scanned his surroundings for the ATVs. He had a rough idea of where the two cars were, but he hadn't seen where the ATVs had run off to, and they were his biggest concern right now. He listened to see if he could pick up the distinct sound of their throaty exhaust nearby, but the only thing he could hear, other than the distant sound of the cars, was his heart thumping wildly in his chest.

Keeping his eyes peeled for any sign of the ATVs, he attempted to reach Fred on the radio.

"Come in, Fred. Do you copy? Over." He tried to be patient and give Fred a few seconds to answer but gave up and repeated the call. This time, as soon as he let go of the button, he was rewarded with a response, although it wasn't the voice he expected.

"Go ahead. Read you loud and clear. Over." Even through the heavy static, Vince instantly recognized the voice as Mary's. He was a little concerned that Fred hadn't answered the call and wondered if everything was all right, but he knew there was no time to get into that now.

"Get everybody ready. Bad guys headed your way. One car, not sure how many people. Over."

"Got it. Are you guys okay? Over."

"Were fine. Can't talk. Get everybody ready now! Over."

"Will do. Over."

The conversation was brief, but that was all there was time for. Vince tried to put Fred's absence out of his mind as he peered over the blackened and paint-peeled hood of the wreck. Immediately, he saw the round shape of the Jeep's headlights headed his way. Looking back over his shoulder, he scanned for any sign of the other car or the ATVs but saw nothing.

He heard gunshots and jerked his head in the other direction. It didn't sound like the AR Tom was using; Vince knew the sound of a .223, and what he heard was something else. Then he heard the familiar crack of Tom's AR and saw the headlights of the car chasing them swerve out from behind the Jeep as it fishtailed and struggled to keep up in the rough median strip.

The looters' sedan looked out of control in the thick grass as it chased the Jeep. John was smart, leading them through the median like that. The Jeep and its knobby tires made easy work of the dirt and overgrown weeds, but the car wasn't made for that type of terrain. It struggled to find traction as the sedan's ill-equipped suspension took a beating on the rough ground, its tires spinning as they failed to find traction in the dirt.

At about thirty yards out, John steered the chase

out of the median, onto the pavement, and toward the wreck that Vince was hiding behind. Vince pulled the pump handle back on the shotgun and swapped out the birdshot with one of the double-aught buckshot shells. They'd be moving quickly when they passed by, and he wanted to make his shot count.

The double-aught buckshot would guarantee the maximum amount of damage, even if he hit the car in a less than desirable spot. The heavy steel shot would easily tear through the sheet metal, and if he wasn't able to take out the driver, he at least hoped to stop the car.

Once on the pavement, the small inline six-cylinder of the Jeep was no match for the old big-block V8 sedan, and the looters began to gain ground on John and Tom. Vince brought the shotgun up to the ready position and braced himself as the vehicles approached.

He took a few deep breaths and tried to determine the timing and how much he should lead the car for the shot. If John led them by his hiding spot at his current distance, he wouldn't need to lead his target by much.

Vince hoped to take out the driver and the passenger with one well-placed shot. He wasn't sure if there were more people than that in the car, but if he took out the driver at this speed, it wouldn't much matter.

SURVIVAL

Vince could hear the roar of the engines now as John steered the Jeep toward the wreck. If the sedan followed his lead, both vehicles would pass him by at less than a few yards. Vince inched his way to the edge of the wreck and crouched behind the trunk. Finger on the trigger, his heart beat rapidly again, but this time it wasn't exhaustion—it was adrenaline.

· 11 ·

Vince caught a glimpse of John's face as the Jeep flew by. The gust of wind it generated sucked particles of ash and soot off the burned-out car and pulled them spiraling up and into the vacuum the Jeep had created. The sedan was in hot pursuit and only lagged behind by a few seconds.

Vince could see the driver and passenger clearly now. They appeared to be the only ones in the car. The driver gripped the wheel with both hands while the passenger brandished a pistol and leaned out of his window. The passenger was focused on taking aim at the Jeep and failed to see Vince as he rose a few inches above the wreck and leaned in for the shot.

The recoil stung Vince's shoulder as the high-powered shell exploded, launching its payload at the speeding sedan. The driver noticed Vince at the last moment, but it was too late. A split second later, the cluster of steel balls tore into the car door, shattering the driver's window into a thousand pieces as they delivered their wrath.

Vince didn't have to wonder if the shot had found its mark, as a fine mist of blood covered the inside of the remaining intact windows. He watched as the sedan continued forward and sped down the road.

John slowed down and turned the Jeep into the median as he let the car fly by. He slowly began to circle back toward Vince as they all kept their attention on the still-speeding sedan.

For a moment, Vince wondered if the driver had somehow survived, as the car showed no signs of slowing; if anything, the car appeared to speed up. Eventually, it began to drift left and head toward the steep embankment of the drainage ditch that ran alongside the roadway. As soon as the wheels reached the soft shoulder, the car swerved violently and disappeared into the ditch, only to reappear a moment later on the other side. Launching itself off the far side of the ditch, it turned over in the air before coming to a roof-crushing stop in the weeds.

Vince stared as the scene seemed to unfold in slow motion. The tires were the only thing still moving when he was finally able to bring himself to look away from the carnage. John pulled up next to Vince; Tom was still in the back.

"You okay?" he asked.

"Yeah. Any sign of the ATVs?" Vince asked.

"Haven't seen 'em," Tom answered as he continued to stare at the overturned car.

Vince was afraid that the ATVs had headed back toward the quarry and would intercept Cy in the loader. He was torn and didn't know what to do. He was also concerned about the other car and the fact that Fred hadn't answered the radio.

Should they continue on into town and help the others at the motel, or should they go back and rejoin Cy? Vince was inclined to do the latter. After all, Cy was alone, and even though he was armed, it would be two against one if the remaining ATV riders found him.

"I got a hold of Mary on the radio," Vince said, climbing into the Jeep. "They know the looters are coming. I think we need to head back and cover Cy."

"I agree, but what happened to Fred?" John asked. "I thought he was on watch duty."

"He was. Maybe he had to take a leak or something. I'm going to try and reach out to them again and see if the other car showed up yet." Vince got settled into his seat and tried the radio. "Come in, Mary. This is Vince. Have you seen the looters yet? Over."

There was a crackle followed by static before Mary's voice broke through the hissing and popping.

"Nothing yet, but we're ready for them. How are you guys making out? Over."

"So far so good. We'll be back ASAP. Over."

Mary didn't answer, or at least it didn't transmit if she had. Vince fooled with the knob on the two-way in an effort to cut down on the static, hoping to get a signal again and hear from Mary, but nothing came through. He had wanted to ask why Fred wasn't manning his post or why Marry had the radio.

"Why isn't it working?" Tom asked.

John shook his head. "Too much interference."

They were headed farther away from Cloverfield now and back toward the quarry, but the radios should have easily worked at this range. Vince wondered if it was due to the thickness of the air or some change the EMPs had caused in the atmosphere. The air quality was slowly improving, but small reflective particles were still visible in the headlights ahead of the Jeep.

Vince couldn't help but wonder what long-term health problems this would create for them. He regretted not bringing the masks with them now, but it was the last thing on his mind when they were preparing to get the loader. But seeing the floating particles highlighted in the Jeep's high beams made him realize how bad it still was. Maybe they had attempted all this too soon. But there was no time to worry about that right now, and he turned his attention to the road ahead, looking for Cy.

He glanced over as they passed the ATV that Tom had taken out. The body was still hunched over the gas tank. The light remained on, but the rifle that had been slung over the rider's body was noticeably missing. The two ATVs that had doubled back must have stopped and taken it.

John continued on, slowing down as they approached the spot where Vince had shot the first looter and blown him off the four-wheeler. The body lay limp and twisted on the shoulder of the road. The shotgun he had been carrying was broken and in pieces on the ground around him.

Vince was disappointed about not being able to retrieve the weapons, but he was at least glad they were both dead and wouldn't cause him and the others any more trouble. Hopefully the other ATV riders had seen that Vince and his crew meant business and decided to return to wherever they had come from.

He was surprised at the lack of guilt he felt for killing the looters. They were bad people and they deserved what they got, but he thought he would feel something. Instead, a feeling of numbness and a total lack of empathy for the looters overwhelmed him, and he just didn't have the energy to care. He was willing to accept that this was the way things were now.

Survival

They hardly noticed the loader on the other side of the highway as they flew past in the opposite direction.

"There he is," Vince shouted. None of the lights were working on the loader—either that or Cy had shut them off.

John hit the brakes and drove across the median as he turned around and caught up to Cy in the southbound lane.

The loader was already stopped, and Cy had the cab door open as they pulled up next to him.

Cy threw up his hands. "The lights stopped working."

"Okay, we'll go slow. Follow us close behind. Did you see any of the looters come back this way?" Vince asked.

"Yeah, I saw 'em. Two of them flew by in a hurry. I don't know if they spotted me or not, but they didn't even slow down."

"We took out one of the cars and the other two ATVs," John said, "but the other car headed into town. We need to hurry up and get back as fast as we can."

"Go on without me. I'll be all right. I've been using my flashlight to see ahead when I need it." Cy held up the small but bright LED light he had taken from his dad's shop.

"We're not leaving you again," Vince said. "We'll go back together. Stay close." He hoped

John and Tom felt the same and looked at both of them after he spoke.

They shook their heads in agreement, and he was glad. If they had wanted to head back without Cy, Vince was prepared to stay with his son and let them go on ahead.

Cy nodded and climbed back inside the cab as John pulled ahead of the loader and headed back to town.

"How fast do you think he can go in that thing?" John asked.

"Thirty is probably the limit in high gear," Vince said, "if it's running right. Let's hope the lights are the only thing not working." He figured Cy had damaged some of the wiring when he hotwired the loader. Hopefully nothing else would be affected. He was certain they could fix them later at his garage; they just had to get there and fast.

There was still another car out there and unaccounted for. When he talked to Mary for the second time on the radio, he was surprised that she hadn't seen them yet. Town was only a few more miles ahead from where they had last seen the car. The looters should have arrived shortly after Vince talked to her the first time, unless they had changed their minds and decided to come back and fight.

"Guys, look." Tom leaned forward, between the seats.

"I see it," John grumbled. Up ahead in the distance, headed toward them, was the single headlight of the black sedan.

· 12 ·

There was no mistaking the single headlight for the black sedan that Vince had shot during the skirmish at the garage. He wasn't happy to see it by any means, but he was glad the looters had decided to come back this way instead of continuing on into town.

Vince was confident in his ability to handle the looters with John and Tom's help. He also had a newfound respect for Tom's ability with the AR. The shot he pulled off on the second ATV was by no means easy. Add in the fact that he made it from a moving vehicle and in these low-light conditions, it was downright impressive—or was it lucky? Vince wanted to believe that Tom's accuracy was due to skill, especially now that the looters were back.

"Well I guess we know where they are now," John said.

Vince glanced back at the loader and waved his hand until he had Cy's attention. He pointed at the oncoming looters and Cy nodded to acknowledge that he saw them, too.

Tom sat up in his seat. "They're headed straight for us on our side of the road."

The car was still too far away to tell how many of them there were. Vince assumed there were at least a couple of looters in the car, if not more. Now he really wished they had an extra radio so he could communicate with Cy in the loader. The looters were most likely ignorant of the fact that they had a ten-ton loader fifty yards behind them, and Vince was already busy trying to think of a way they could use that to their advantage. Of course, he also didn't want to put Cy in danger.

"I'm guessing they're going to try and force us off the road," Vince said. "Maybe you can get to them before they get to us, Tom."

"I'll do my best." Tom climbed back up into his position over the roll bar and steadied himself in the wind. They weren't going as fast as when he took out the ATV, but finding the target was a long shot in the dark and with open sights.

Before Tom could fire on them, Vince saw a flash of light from the side of the oncoming sedan. A split second later, the sound of a bullet whizzing by caught everyone's attention.

"They're shooting at us!" John began to weave back and forth across the road in an effort to make them a tougher target to hit. Vince loaded another round of double-aught buckshot into the shotgun, although they were still too far away for the shotgun to be effective.

Again, a flash of light lit up the passenger side of the sedan, followed by the whistle of another stray bullet, only this time it sounded closer.

"Any time you want to return fire would be great, Tom," John yelled out.

Tom didn't answer with words and instead squeezed off two rounds from the AR in short succession. The single headlight almost immediately swerved toward the median but, seemingly unfazed by the shots, jerked back to the center of the road.

The distance between the jeep and sedan was shrinking fast, and it was clear that the sedan was going much faster than the jeep. John had only sped up a little from the thirty miles per hour or so they were maintaining for Cy's sake.

Vince was surprised to see Tom sit down on the back seat and put the AR in his lap.

"What are you doing, man? Return fire!" Vince barked.

"The gun. It's jammed." Tom was frantically pulling and pushing the charging handle back and forth. Vince could see that there was casing stuck in the action, and it was crimped. Suddenly, Vince regretted not inspecting the guns he had pulled off the dead looters. This was one of the ARs he'd taken from the guy he shot at the garage, and there was no telling when it had last been cleaned or how well it had been taken care of.

He took the gun from Tom and inspected it with his flashlight. Confirming what he feared, the shiny brass shell casing had jammed in the action and was wedged in too tight to move with his fingers. He thought about grabbing a pair of pliers from the tool bag but remembered it was with Cy. He was about to grab his pocket knife to try and pry the jammed casing out when he looked to check the distance between him and the sedan. The approaching car was too close now; there was no time to sort the gun out.

John had one hand on the wheel and his Glock drawn in the other.

"Just get down." Vince tossed the AR back to Tom and grabbed hold of the shotgun. The looters were headed straight for them in a deadly game of chicken. There was no telling which way they would swerve, but if they went to the left, Vince would have no clear shot at them without running the risk of hitting John.

CRACK! The loud noise caught Vince off guard, and he instinctively pulled away from the windshield as hundreds of hairline cracks spider-webbed out from a bullet hole that appeared near the bottom of the frame. John swerved to the right at the last second, and the sedan went left. The tires on the Jeep squealed, and Vince could have sworn they were on two wheels for a moment as the two vehicles missed each other by less than a couple of feet.

Vince glanced back and saw that there was a passenger in the back seat as well, and he was leaning out the busted rear window and taking aim at the Jeep with a pistol.

"Look out!" Vince yelled as John struggled to recover control of the skidding Jeep. Tom was down low and hugging the seat in an attempt to hang on, and Vince realized he was in the greatest danger of being hit by the gunman. But before the shooter could fire his weapon, the sedan swerved again, this time hard to the right, throwing the back-seat passenger to the side and out of sight.

Vince realized the reason for the sudden turn and watched in amazement as the loader struck the car broadside. The deafening metallic bang was followed by the distinct noise of crumpling steel. The remaining windows shattered as the whole car shuddered under the tremendous force of the impact. The partially raised bucket ripped into the car like a cheap aluminum can and tore both passenger doors completely off. The momentum of the blow sent the remainder of the sedan into a violent lateral roll that ejected one of the passengers on its second time around. It rolled twice more before grinding to a halt on the pavement, leaving a trail of fluids behind it.

Cy brought the loader to a stop just short of running over what was left of the mangled and twisted vehicle. John circled back, parked next to the loader, and fixed the Jeep's headlights on the scene.

"Holy crap!" Tom stood up on the back seat and surveyed the carnage, but Vince had seen the impact and was worried about Cy. He leaped from the Jeep, raced up the ladder to the cab of the loader, and yanked the door open in one swift motion.

"Cy, are you okay?"

"Um... Yeah, I think so." Cy was clearly dazed by the collision and was unaware he had a small trickle of blood running down his forehead.

"You're bleeding." Vince inspected the cut.

"What? I am?" As he came to his senses, Cy put his hand to his head and then pulled it away to see the blood.

"It doesn't look too bad. Just a small cut." Vince continued to inspect it with his flashlight. "I'll drive the loader the rest of the way back. Why don't you take it easy and ride back in the Jeep?"

"Yeah... Okay," Cy agreed. Vince climbed down and held out his hand to help Cy out of the cab.

"I got it," Cy said.

Once on the ground, the two joined John and Tom, who were out of the Jeep and inspecting the leaking car. A puddle of fluids had accumulated around the front end of the mangled sedan, and John was crouched down, trying to get a better look inside the vehicle. He stood up slowly and looked at Cy, shaking his head.

"Well, Cy, you certainly did a number on them. And not a second too soon. That was close."

"Yeah, too close," Tom added. But Cy's attention was focused on the twisted remains of the passenger who was thrown from the vehicle. The body lay in an expanding pool of blood not more than twenty feet from the wreck. Vince recognized the man's shirt and knew it was the gunman from the back seat. He looked around to see if he could spot the pistol, but it was nowhere to be seen.

"Ah...guys, we might want to get away from the car." Tom stepped back as a small fire broke out and began to quickly spread near the front of the car.

"Yeah, let's get going." Vince put his hand on Cy's shoulder and gently pulled him toward the Jeep and away from the body. Fire or not, Vince was anxious to get back. Somewhere, there were still two unaccounted-for ATVs with armed riders.

It seemed like the other looters had fled, but they'd seen enough action for one night and he didn't want to push his luck. He also didn't want to risk them coming back with reinforcements.

· 13 ·

Vince made sure Cy got into the Jeep all right before he took over in the loader.

"I'll follow you guys back. Don't forget I don't have any lights," Vince reminded John.

"No problem. Nice and easy," John replied.

Once up in the cab, Vince noticed that the sedan's two passenger-side doors were still attached to the loader, where they had been impaled by the row of ten-inch steel teeth along the leading edge of the bucket. Vince fooled with the controls a bit as John began to pull away. Once he had it figured out, he dropped the bucket down until the doors made contact with the road. Then he put the loader in reverse. He could hear the metal scraping the asphalt as he moved backward until the doors were free of the loader's bucket.

Careful to steer clear of the doors and any other debris from the wreck, he followed the Jeep back toward Cloverdale. He was sure to glance over his shoulder every so often in case the ATVs returned. He doubted they would, but he wasn't taking any chances. They'd pushed their luck far enough tonight.

With the loader in high gear, he could easily maintain a steady twenty-five miles per hour without incurring too much bounce or pushing the old machine over what he felt was an unnecessary strain on the engine. They needed the loader, and after what they had just been through to get it, he wanted to go easy and avoid a breakdown. He did notice how sensitive the steering was and realized why Cy had almost lost control earlier on the way out of the quarry. He focused on the lights of the Jeep and paid close attention to their path, doing his best to mirror them and avoid the few obstacles they passed on the road. It was slow going, but it was progress, and he was content with the fact that there was no sign of the looters. It seemed the worst was over for the time being.

Vince felt a sense of relief as the faint profile of his garage and the motel up ahead came into view. He wasn't sure if the air was clearing or if he was just happy to be back and elated to have accomplished their task, but the air quality near town seemed a little better than when they left.

Tomorrow would mark the fourth day since the EMPs went off, and Vince couldn't help but feel disappointed in their progress. In his head, he had ideas and plans he'd hoped to have begun implementing by now. But he hadn't planned on the fires taking so long to dissipate.

He had no illusions about the EMPs and how they would continue to impact their lives for quite some time, but he thought the air would clear much faster than it had. The low, dark cloud that lingered over town felt permanent, and the long, twisted trails of still-rising smoke seemed to be holding it in place. There had been little to no wind—or weather for that matter—in the last couple of days, and the air was heavy with dust particles and soot.

He wondered if the high-altitude detonations had somehow changed the atmosphere. He wasn't educated in those things, though, and could only speculate how or if the EMPs could affect the weather. It certainly felt different and unusually hot and dry for this early in the summer. At this time of year, he would have expected to see rain at least once in the past few days.

But the air had a dryness to it that reminded him of winter without the biting cold. He even noticed that the grass and weeds along the side of the road had begun to turn an unhealthy shade of brown. Some had already succumbed to the drought-like conditions and had withered and died, reminding him that growing food for themselves might not be an easy task without constant irrigation.

Providing water to crops would be yet another task to add to his growing list of things the town would need to do in order to survive. Nothing would come easily, and the everyday things they had taken for granted before would now be out of reach without hard work.

Vince tried to push the growing list from his mind as the tasks that lay ahead started to overwhelm his thoughts. He tried to focus on the fact that they would have to take it one day at a time and one task at a time.

They had the loader now and that was a huge win for them. It would make clearing the roads possible and it would fast-track their efforts to protect themselves. Defending their position, which right now consisted of the motel and the garage, was the priority.

Vince wasn't sure how many of the looters' gang was left, but he was sure they wouldn't let up with the attacks until they had succeeded in taking what they wanted or Vince and the others had taken them all out. It was still hard to believe that their lives had deteriorated to this level of desperation in such a short time, but they had, and that was just the way it was going to be from now on.

Vince followed the Jeep to the motel but veered off along the sidewalk by the street instead of pulling into the parking lot behind John. He was tired but anxious to build a temporary barrier across the road into town. He really wished the lights were working and ultimately decided that he'd work on that right away rather than put it off until morning. As much as he wanted to sleep, the town's security was more important. If Cy helped him, maybe they could make short work of the repairs.

Vince put the loader in neutral and left it running. He didn't want to go through the effort of untwisting the wires if he was going to drive it over to the garage and work on it, but he did want to take a minute and check in on the others. He was also curious to see why Fred had abandoned his watch duties and left Mary to fill in.

As John pulled into the motel and parked in front of the row of rooms, the others came out and assembled around the Jeep. Vince headed over to join the crown and was met by an overenthusiastic Nugget, who proceeded to wiggle around at his feet as he walked.

"All right, girl, it's good to see you, too." Vince reached down and gave her a few scratches on her head before she ran back to Mary.

There were hugs and handshakes all around as the others welcomed them back. Everyone smiled when they saw the loader and realized that the mission had been a success.

"Where's Fred?" Vince asked.

Mary's smile faded. "He got sick and I took over for him. Reese is in their room with him now. He started vomiting and said he had a really bad headache."

Vince's thoughts immediately went to the possibility of radiation poisoning. Would he eventually get sick as well? What about Cy and Reese and her mom, Hannah? They were all exposed to the same level of radiation. They were all close to the blast in Indianapolis.

His mind raced, and he felt his blood pressure rise as thoughts of impending doom filled his head. He tried to think of other possibilities, like the lack of sleep and the fact that they had been eating poorly. There was also the number of toxins they were breathing in on a daily basis. Even though they were trying to be careful and take preventative measures when they could, it was unavoidable.

He forced himself to slow down and stop jumping to conclusions about their health. It wouldn't do any good to get himself or anyone else worked up about the thought of radiation poisoning. It'd be a good idea to give everyone another round of the potassium iodine pills if there were enough. He'd have to talk to Reese about that privately. He didn't want to alarm anybody, but Reese was a smart girl and he was sure she had already thought about the possibility.

Survival

Vince stood back as Cy and Tom answered questions and filled the others in about their adventure. Vince was too tired and focused on what still needed to be done, and he really didn't feel like talking about it. Over the last few days, he had been forced to kill people, and while he understood there wasn't any other option, it overshadowed the feeling of accomplishment the others expressed in securing the loader.

He also noticed that in the excitement, John had slipped off unnoticed and disappeared back into his room. The adrenaline rush of what they had done had certainly worn off, and John was most likely consumed by the guilt and sadness of having lost his family. Vince couldn't imagine how he felt and knew it would take time. He thought about going after him but decided to leave the man alone and give him some space. If the shoe were on the other foot, that was what Vince would want.

There was nothing he could do for Fred, either, and was sure Reese had the situation handled as best as she could. The most he could do right now was to fix the lights on the loader and start building a barricade.

For now, he would use what was close by and available. There were enough burned-out wrecks and debris lying around to throw together a formidable blockade. It would be temporary, but it would buy them extra time in case of another attack and would also serve to take away the looters' ability to terrorize them from their vehicles. It would, at the very least, put them on a level playing field for their next encounter.

· 14 ·

As the group started to break up, Cy noticed his dad and Mary walking slowly toward the edge of the parking lot. Nugget was close behind, sniffing hard at the ground as she followed.

Cy broke away from the group and moved toward them. He got there just in time to see Mary give his dad a hug and climb into the Ford pickup. She made room for Nugget to join her and smiled at Cy as she closed the door behind the eager little dog.

"I guess Mary is going to take a shift?" Cy asked.

"Yeah, she'll trade off with Bill in a couple hours. You feel up to helping me out with the loader? I want to get the lights working so I can set up a roadblock before we call it a night."

"Sure. It's probably just some loose wires." Cy shrugged. "I might have been a little too aggressive when I pulled the ignition wires out. It was hard to see."

Vince looked at his forehead. "I thought you were going to get Reese to look at that?"

Cy had forgotten all about it and rubbed at the dried blood on his head. "She's got her hands full. Besides, it's fine. Just a scratch."

"All right. Well, just make sure you clean it out tonight before you go to bed." Vince climbed into the loader.

"I will." Cy wondered sometimes if his dad would ever stop treating him like a kid.

"Hop in the bucket. I'll give you a ride this time. It'll be a whole lot easier to work on this thing over at the garage." Vince raised the bucket off the ground a couple of feet and Cy jumped in. It was a short, bumpy ride over to his dad's garage, and Cy hopped out before the loader came to a complete stop in front of the far-left overhead door that led to the empty garage bay.

His dad tossed him the keys, and he quickly unlocked the building. Using his flashlight, he made his way through the storefront and to the garage bay, where he unlocked both slide bolts and lifted the overhead door. Stepping off to the side and out of the way, he made room for his dad to pull the loader inside. The top of the cab cleared the door header by less than a foot.

"Tight fit," Cy yelled over the amplified sound of the diesel engine as the old John Deere rolled inside the building. Once the loader was clear of the door, his dad reached down and untwisted the wires. The diesel sputtered and then went quiet inside the dark garage, except for a slight ringing in Cy's ears. He flicked his flashlight back on and shined it up at the cab. "What tools do you want?"

"I think we may have to break down and run some lights, just for a little while, but it might make this go a little faster." Vince climbed down and disappeared into the back room. He reappeared a minute later and flicked the switch on the wall.

The fluorescent light fixture directly above the loader hummed and then flickered a couple of times before remaining on. The unnatural white light washed over the loader and spilled onto the oil-stained concrete floor. It took a second for Cy's eyes to adjust as he stared at the light, unable to look away even though he knew better. The brightness of the light and the contrast of the sharp shadow lines inside the garage were surreal and seemed strangely out of place. It had been a while since he'd seen that much artificial light.

"Your eyes are better than mine," Vince said. "Want to take a look and see if you can figure it out? You did a pretty good job gettin' her started."

"Sure thing." Cy suddenly felt guilty for thinking his dad was treating him like a kid earlier when he nagged him about the cut on his head. But more than that, he was proud that his dad trusted him to try and fix the lights.

"Well, you know it's not my first time messing around with a loader like this." Cy figured now was as good a time as any to let his dad know about the incident at his mom's. Not that he had to tell him, but he felt like he should for some reason.

"Oh, really? You worked on one of these before?" Vince asked.

"Not so much worked on one but kind of...um...borrowed one, I guess you could say." Cy jumped into the cab and hid his face under the console. All of a sudden, Cy regretted bringing it up, but it was too late to go back now.

"Borrowed?" Vince asked. Cy proceeded to tell his dad about what he and his friends had done so many years ago and how they got in trouble for it and his mom had promised never to tell his dad. Cy was surprised to hear his dad chuckle when he finished the story.

Vince sighed. "Yeah, your mom told me about that but made me promise not to let on that I knew anything."

"Oh." Cy was embarrassed and a little relieved to get it off his chest, but the feeling was quickly replaced by sadness as thoughts of his mother filled his head. He'd thought about her off and on over the last couple of days, along with his ex-girlfriend, Kate. All the sitting around the motel room and waiting for things to settle down and the smoke to clear left a lot of time for thinking—too much time.

Survival

He'd gone back and forth, convincing himself several times that his mom and Kate were both still alive and then telling himself that they hadn't made it. Cy had practically driven himself crazy by running through the possible scenarios in his mind. This was one of the reasons why he was eager to help go and find the loader. Anything was better than staring at the wall in his room.

"So that was pretty crazy, huh?" Cy said, eager to change the subject. "I can't believe they came after us like that."

"Well, to be honest, I kind of expected it. I actually thought the looters would've shown up long before now, especially after the last run-in," Vince admitted.

"I guess this is going to be a regular thing, then."

"Unfortunately, yes. I imagine it's only going to get worse as they get more desperate. Not to mention they have a score to settle with us," Vince added.

"It's hard to believe all that's happened in the past few days. It doesn't even seem real. At least parts of it, anyway." The truth was, some of what had happened seemed too real—like the terrified faces of the people in the sedan right before impact with the loader. That was real, and it bothered him. Cy found the wires he suspected of causing the lights to malfunction and reached into the bag for the electrical tape. "There is a part of me that feels bad for the looters and a part of me that feels like they got what they deserved," he added.

"There's no reason to feel guilty about protecting yourself and others. Don't ever feel bad about that. We all did what had to be done back there and the last time they attacked. They brought this on themselves."

"I know, but it's hard to think about. Part of me is still in denial about what is happening around us. How can so much change so quickly?" Cy asked.

Vince cleared his throat. "I know. There's nothing easy about any of this. I'm just glad I have you here with me. I don't know what I'd do without you, Cy."

Cy looked down at his dad. "I'm glad I'm here, too, Dad." He paused for a second and considered leaving it at that, but he wanted to let his dad know what was on his mind. "If things ever settle down to the point where it's reasonable to travel, I want to go look for Mom and Kate. I know the chances are slim, but I feel like it's something I have to do."

His dad stared at him in silence for a few seconds and then began to slowly nod as he let out a deep breath. "I understand."

· 15 ·

As Cy finished up with the wiring, Vince mulled over what his son had just confessed to him. It wasn't something Vince hadn't considered, but he knew in his gut that the topic would come up. He knew how much Kate meant to Cy and wondered how long it would be before he gave in to his feelings for her and wanted to go after her and his mom.

For the moment, that seemed to be all that Cy wanted to say about the subject, and for the rest of the time in the garage, they mainly made small talk. Vince wanted to try and talk him out of it, but he didn't want to risk getting into an argument. In spite of the circumstances, he was enjoying this time with his son and also didn't want to ruin that over something that might or might not happen.

It would be a long time before it was safe or even possible to travel. For the time being, just going short distances was risky. If there were bad people here around Cloverdale, it was safe to assume there were worse people in other places. Vince shuddered as he thought about the possible conditions in and around some of the bigger cities. He imagined some of the scenes likely unfolding around the country and had to force himself to stop.

Vince liked to think that, for the most part, people were decent and good, but he couldn't ignore or deny the reality of what was happening here in their little town. It only took a small group to wreak havoc.

While Cy finished up with the lights, Vince occupied himself by rummaging through some old parts he had lying around and found a simple rocker switch that he thought they could use. If they connected the ignition wires to the switch, they could start and stop the loader that way.

He took it up to Cy in the cab and helped him mount it. They had the wires connected in no time and were ready to test their work.

"Well, cross your fingers. Here goes nothing." Cy flipped the switch. The diesel engine coughed and then roared to life. Cy pulled the knob that controlled the loader's lights and nearly blinded them as the spotlights reflected off the garage wall in front of them.

"Whoa, that's bright!" Cy pushed the knob back in and all was dark again, except for the ceiling light that seemed very dim now in comparison. Vince wasn't sure if the ceiling light only seemed dim because the loader's lights had just blasted them or if the power reserves were getting low. Either way, it was time to shut the breaker off to the solar panels; they had used enough electricity already.

Vince went back to the panel box and secured the breaker to the solar panels for the night. By the time he returned to the garage, Cy had pulled the loader out into the parking lot and was closing the large overhead garage door. Vince helped him finish locking the place up, and they stopped in the storefront long enough to grab a few things before heading back outside.

"Why don't you go get that cleaned up?" Vince said. "I'm going to throw up a quick blockade across the road. It shouldn't take me too long."

"You sure you don't want some help?" Cy asked. "I could do it if you want."

"No. I got it. It's kind of a one-man job anyway."

"Fine, have it your way, old man," Cy joked.

"Yeah, yeah. I hear ya. You want a ride back?" Vince asked.

"No thanks. I'll walk. That bucket isn't exactly luxury seating." Cy rolled his eyes and started for the motel. Vince climbed into the running loader and closed the door to the cab as he watched Cy walk across the street. It really was a miracle that his plane landed early on Sunday and that they both survived the blast. It was pretty bad right now, but all things considered, it could have been a lot worse.

Vince didn't want to think about how close he'd come to losing his son and threw the loader into gear. It was time to get to work; he was tired but motivated and in a small way looking forward to using the big machine. After what they'd been through already with the looters, he was glad to finally be taking some proactive measures to help ensure their survival.

He headed north and away from town for about a hundred yards before he came to a spot that looked like a good place to construct the roadblock. A burned-out delivery truck had already ended up nose-first in the ditch with its body extending across the shoulder and part of the southbound lane. Directly across from the truck, on the other side of the road, there was a steep ditch with a tight cluster of pine trees at the top of the far bank.

This would be a good spot to build the barricade; it was a natural choke point and it wouldn't take much to fill in the remaining gaps. Not too far in either direction, there were a couple of wrecks that wouldn't have to be moved very far.

The first car he tried to lift with the loader didn't want to cooperate, and every time he would get the bucket partway under and try to scoop the car up, it would simply slide forward and fall out. After several unsuccessful attempts to lift the car and carry it, he decided the best method would be to simply push the vehicles and use the loader like a glorified bulldozer. It wasn't how he had imagined this working, but it would get the job done for now.

He began thinking of ways to modify the bucket and make it easier to carry the wrecks. Pushing wouldn't always work, especially if he wanted to stack some of the cars and make a more formidable roadblock. Vince had a welder at his shop, and he wondered if he could weld a pair of forks onto the bucket and make it more like a forklift.

He knew they made attachments like that for construction equipment used for moving pallets of heavy material. Maybe the quarry had an attachment like that. Before he permanently welded something on, it might be worth having a look. The idea of going back out there seemed like a bad one right now, so he'd make due. If they returned to the quarry, they'd be sure to go during the daytime, if Vince had anything to say about it.

He pushed the last car into place and was satisfied that at least the road was unusable. Sure, the looters could go around through the fields, but it wouldn't be easy, at least not for the cars. The ATVs would be able to get in more easily, but short of a complete wall, this was the best he could do right now. He still liked the idea of taking vehicles from the local dealership and using them for a barricade, but that would be no small undertaking, and for right now, this was better than nothing.

It was going to be a pain to have to use the loader to move the cars every time they wanted to leave town this way, but he didn't see a need to go back out on this road for a while. His immediate plan was to focus on clearing the roads in town, finding the houses and buildings that hadn't been destroyed, and searching for supplies.

Vince headed back to the motel in the loader; he was beat and was looking forward to lying down for the night. Hopefully the looters had gotten their fill of terrorizing for one night and would leave them alone for a while. Both times they'd managed to hold their ground and the looters had suffered casualties. Vince was pretty sure he and the other survivors had presented a sufficient reason for them to stay away for the time being. Both times they attacked had been at night, and he wondered if their courage was alcohol-fueled or if they were just that bloodthirsty.

Either way, the looters would be back as supplies dwindled. And the more established he and the others became, the bigger target they would become. There were only so many stores and homes to pillage; stealing supplies wasn't a sustainable way to survive.

But right now, they all needed rest so they could hit it early tomorrow. The air was improving enough to start working on the projects and ideas he had. They needed to drive out to Mary's house and eventually his place. He had talked to Mary about rounding up her chickens and other animals and bringing them to the motel. The motel building was built in the shape of a square and had a landscaped center courtyard—the perfect place to keep her livestock. They could easily gate off the access points to the courtyard and keep the animals contained.

With the animals she had, they would have fresh eggs from the chickens and ducks and milk from the goats. She had three pigs, and while they could be a great food source, butchering them would be shortsighted. They needed to keep them healthy and, with any luck, produce piglets. A sow could give birth to a litter of seven to twelve piglets twice a year with a gestation period of a little over three months. It would be an investment in feed and time, but if it worked and they were smart about it, they would have enough to sustain their small group for a long time.

He just hoped all of her animals had survived. When they left her house, they had no idea that they would be gone for so long. Mary had high hopes, though, and said that all the animals had access to her barn and plenty of feed. Her biggest concern was for the pigs, but the chickens, ducks, and goats could find food on their own without too much trouble.

In fact, the more he thought about it, the more he was sure that tomorrow they should make retrieving her animals a priority. Energy bars and sports drinks were getting old and wreaking havoc on their digestive systems. The other things they were eating, like the crackers, chips, and candy bars from his little store, weren't much better. They needed real food—and soon.

Outside of Mary's animals and what they could provide for their group, the only other viable options would be limited. Growing produce and hunting would be the only way to sustain themselves. Vince was fairly confident that they could take a deer a week from his property alone, but it wouldn't do any good if they couldn't keep the meat from spoiling.

The motel had a couple of large chest freezers in the kitchen area, but they had no way to power them until they ran some lines from the garage. Even then, running the freezers at that distance and around the clock would be a strain on the garage's solar power system. Part of his plan was to eventually supply the motel with power, but he saw it being more of an occasional thing, and it probably wouldn't be available at all times. Maybe a couple of hours in the morning or at night—enough to provide some creature comforts and keep everyone motivated.

It would be better to drag the chest freezers over to the garage and set them up over there. He could easily isolate a dedicated line to them and keep them running much more efficiently than he could at the motel, not to mention he could keep an eye on things better at the garage and lock them up in the back room. It wasn't that he didn't trust anyone in his group right now, but they were sure to find other survivors as the community grew, so it would be simpler this way.

Vince thought about tucking the loader away inside the garage for the night but decided that with someone on watch at all times, there would be no harm in parking it outside the motel. He pulled up to the curb and noticed Cy outside, talking to Mary in the pickup.

He shut the loader off using the newly installed switch and started over to the truck. As he approached, Nugget became excited and fogged up the truck window with her breath in anticipation. Vince looked around and saw a couple of the rooms dimly lit by the lanterns he'd handed out the other day. For the first time in a while, he felt a small amount of relief and comfort as he took in his surroundings and what had become their new home.

· 16 ·

Vince stopped at the pickup to talk to Mary and Cy for a minute and give Nugget a few scratches on the head. He was also glad to see that Cy had heeded his advice and finally cleaned the cut on his head.

"How's Fred doing? Any change?" Vince asked.

"I talked to Reese and she said he's doing a little better. At least he stopped vomiting and is sleeping now," Cy answered.

"Good. How are you doing, Mary? Hanging in there?" Vince asked.

"Yeah, I'm fine. Bill's going to relieve me at twelve. That's a nice little roadblock you made there." Mary looked out at the road and admired his handiwork.

"Thanks. It won't stop anybody, but it'll sure slow them down."

"You look tired. Why don't you go get some rest? Everything's under control out here." Mary reached through the window and put her hand on Vince's arm. She was right on both counts, and there really wasn't anything else for him to do right now. Vince nodded and started for the room but stopped and looked back at Cy.

"You should get some rest, too, Cy. It's going to be a big day tomorrow."

"I'm right behind you." Cy gave Nugget a few final rubs before stepping out of the truck, and he quickly caught up to his dad on the way back to the room.

"What's the plan for tomorrow?" Cy asked.

"Well, I'd like to get started clearing off the roadways so we can get around town and check for any more survivors. We also need to gather up any supplies that made it through the fires. And while we're doing all that, I'd like to get out to Mary's and gather her animals. Hopefully most of them made it through this."

"What about the looters? Do you think they'll come back?"

"More than likely, but we can't let that get in our way. I don't want to sit around waiting for another attack."

"But we'll at least have to leave some people back here to guard the place, right?"

"Definitely, but with the radios and if we work in groups, we'll be fine. Maybe you can help me in the morning over at the garage. After we top off the water containers, I want to weld some forks onto the loader bucket if there is enough power left in the reserves."

"Yeah, no problem. I can give you a hand with that." Cy headed off toward his room and turned back toward Vince.

"Dad?"

"Yeah?"

"About what I said before, about going to look for Mom and Kate. I want you to know I'm not planning on doing that for a while. I'll be here to help out for as long as you need me."

Vince was glad to hear Cy say those words. Ever since he mentioned his intentions to go back to Washington, it had been weighing heavily on Vince. He had wanted to ask Cy for more details, especially about the timing of it all, but he really didn't know what to say or how to ask.

"Good. I'm glad to hear that. Having you here is a huge asset. I don't know what I'd do without you, son."

Cy smiled and turned toward his room. "Goodnight, Dad."

"Goodnight." Vince watched Cy disappear into his room. He felt like a weight had been lifted from his chest. He was worried Cy was planning on taking off in the next few days or something like that. At least he was being realistic about his plans. Maybe he wouldn't end up going at all, although

Vince doubted that very much and he didn't intend to talk him out of it.

Vince also knew that this meant he would probably end up going with him. There was no way he could let him make a trip like that alone. The dangers he would face out there in this post-apocalyptic world would be too much for one person to handle on his own.

Maybe things would improve sooner than he thought. Maybe within a week or so the grid would be restored and they'd all be surprised by a convoy of Army National Guardsmen rolling into town to restore law and order. Vince had to laugh under his breath. Now he was the one who wasn't being realistic. He knew no such event would happen, at least not any time soon.

Cloverdale wasn't even on anybody's map when it came to places to save. The government would have bigger fish to fry—that was one thing he was certain of. It wouldn't waste its resources on a hiccup in the road like Cloverdale. The bigger cities would receive assistance first, and it would take a long time to get places like Indianapolis under control. Vince was willing to bet those places would never be the same again. He could only imagine the chaos they were in right now.

Once inside the room, he plopped down into one of the chairs at the front of the room and looked out the window. He couldn't really see anything, but he stared just the same. Too tired to look away, he finally worked up the energy to peel off his boots and let them fall to the floor, where they kicked up a small cloud of soot and dust from the carpet. He forced himself to get up from his seat and drink some water before brushing his teeth and cleaning the grime from his face. He looked at the towel when he was done cleaning up and was disgusted by the amount of dirt on it. It was a reminder of just how bad it still was outside. The smoke was better than it had been and the air quality was improving, but there was a long way to go yet before he would consider it healthy to breathe.

Once he finished up in the bathroom, he lay down on the bed and felt the tension ease in his aching joints and muscles. He was even more exhausted than he realized, but he felt a little better now that he was clean—or at least as clean as any of them could be right now without running water. It was enough to make him reconsider tomorrow's priorities, and he thought maybe instead he should work on powering the motel. As nice as it would be to have a hot shower, he knew it wasn't time yet. Besides, there wouldn't be enough power for everyone to get cleaned up, so why bother? No, he needed to stick to the original plan.

Vince ran over the watch schedule in his mind and worked out that his next four-hour shift in the rotation wouldn't happen until tomorrow after lunch, and for that, he was thankful. He thought about Fred and really hoped he was feeling better soon. They couldn't afford to be down a man and expect to accomplish everything Vince had planned. Maybe if Fred was still feeling poorly he could take Vince's shift sitting in the pickup and keeping an eye out for looters. That would be easy on Fred and allow Vince to keep working on his projects.

With thoughts of tomorrow still spinning in his head, he felt his eyes begin to grow heavy and drifted off to sleep.

· 17 ·

For the first time since the bombs hit, Vince slept through the night. The pale-yellow light that filtered through the window was a welcome sight and gave him hope that the dark cloud hanging over town had dissipated even more. He looked over at Mary's bed and saw that she was still sleeping, Nugget curled up at the foot of the bed.

Vince rubbed his face and stretched as he tried to work out the soreness in his back and muscles. He felt rested for a change and was surprised to see that it was nearly six in the morning already. He found it hard to believe that he had slept straight through the night, something that was not normal for him even under good circumstances.

He slowly pulled himself out of bed and quietly filled the small coffee pot with water before lighting the portable camp stove. There was plenty to do today, but nothing was going to happen until he had a hot cup of coffee in his hand. Once the coffee was started, he headed into the bathroom with his flashlight and closed the door so as not to wake up Mary while he brushed his teeth.

He stared at his reflection in the mirror and couldn't deny how rough he looked. There were still traces of soot and dirt on his face from yesterday, and it seemed to accentuate the wrinkles around his eyes, making him look older than he wanted to admit. It had been a while since he'd gone this long without shaving, and his all-white beard wasn't helping him feel any younger, either.

He wiped at his face with a damp towel, but at this point, he wasn't sure if he was removing dirt or adding it. They had been careful to conserve what towels and washcloths they had, but they were running out of clean linens.

If they powered the motel, they'd also be able to do laundry—something they all desperately needed to do. He was fortunate that he kept a change of clothes at the garage, but even with that, he felt filthy. The others were all wearing the same clothes they had on since the start of all this. Only Reese and Cy had clothes, because they had been traveling when the EMPs hit.

Vince knew how important it was to keep up with personal hygiene as a means of maintaining morale. It was amazing how much the ability to get clean could impact a person's well-being, not to mention that of the people around him. He imagined no one was complaining because they were all equally offensive at this point.

He flicked off the flashlight and gave up cleaning himself any further. It was probably a waste anyway and he didn't want to dwell on it any longer. A percolating coffee pot beckoned to him from the other room. The familiar aroma made him forget about everything else for a moment. Waiting by the stove impatiently until there was enough coffee brewed to fill his cup, he watched Mary sleep. She looked peaceful, unaware of the danger of this new world—until of course she woke up and was faced with reality once more.

He filled his cup as soon as there was enough and took a small sip of the steaming-hot liquid. He instantly felt better and was reluctant to set the cup down on the table as he pulled on his boots. He exited the room as quietly as he could, but he still managed to wake Nugget as the door creaked open. The little dog wagged her tail and then stopped, disappointed as he began to close the door.

"Oh, all right. Come on, then," Vince whispered. Her tail immediately resumed as her head shot up from the bed. Nugget stood up and stretched quickly before launching off the bed and shooting between his legs and out the door. Happy to be outside, she found a place to relieve herself among some bushes before trotting around the parking lot, sniffing the ground as she went.

Survival

Vince was pleasantly surprised to feel a slight breeze, albeit a warm one, and he noticed the air seemed a little clearer than it had last night. It was still dry and hot for this time in the morning, but it was an improvement. It gave him hope for the day. Maybe things would start to get better. There was still a lack of dew on the ground, but that was how it had been the last couple of mornings, so he wasn't surprised by that.

Vince kept one eye on Nugget as he headed over to the pickup to chat with Bill. As a group, they decided the other day that whoever pulled the midnight watch shift would stay on until six in the morning rather than being relieved by the next person at four. This way, whoever took over at six could have an extra two hours of sleep and whoever had the mid-watch could get some rest and sleep until noon if they needed to. It was better than having two people tired from standing watch all night.

Vince was glad to see Bill wide awake. He actually had the window down in the truck, another sign that the air quality was improving. He would have been disappointed if Bill was sleeping on watch, but he really couldn't have blamed the guy. It was boring and hot out. With no radio to listen to and nothing to do, it was a monotonous task at best.

"Mornin'."

Bill jumped. "Oh, hey, Major. You scared me. I didn't even see you over there."

"How's it going out here?" Vince asked.

"Good. Ready to be relieved. I think the light's playing tricks on my eyes. I keep seeing something out in that far field, but I don't see anything when I look with the binoculars." Bill handed Vince the binoculars and pointed to a field beyond the roadblock. Vince surveyed the area in question for a little while but didn't see anything.

"Nothing." Vince handed the binoculars back to Bill. It's probably just shadows or something. He wasn't overly concerned and knew how things could take on a life of their own at that hour. He thought about all the times he'd been hunting early in the morning and seen a suspicious shape or shadow only to have it turn into a stump or a bush when the sun came up all the way. Plus, there was a breeze blowing the taller weeds around. Add in the fact that Bill had been up since midnight, and he could see how it would be easy to mistake something in the low light.

"Who's your replacement?" Vince asked.

"My wife should be out any minute. She's got the six to ten this morning."

"You going to be able to get any sleep if Sarah is on watch and you have to take care of your daughter?" Vince asked.

"Oh, it's fine. Hannah is going to watch the kids this morning."

"Okay, sounds like you guys have it all worked out. Any word on Fred?"

"No, nothing new. Last I heard, he was feeling a little better and at least sleeping, but I haven't seen anybody all night."

Vince looked at his watch. "All right. Well, hang in there. It's almost six. I'm gonna head over to the garage."

"Okay, Major. Talk to you later." Bill tipped his hat. Vince was about to leave when he heard Nugget whining to be let back into their room. He'd all but forgotten the little dog was out here. Thank goodness she hadn't wandered off. Mary would never forgive him if he lost track of Nugget.

He cracked the door open just enough for Nugget to squeeze in and far enough for him to peek in and see that Mary was still asleep. No point in waking anyone up just yet. The more rest they got, the better off they would be—they certainly deserved it. The only thing he planned on doing right now was looking around the garage for suitable material to build forks for the loader, and he didn't need any help doing that.

Vince headed across the street, toward the garage, nodding at Bill as he passed him. He hoped his wife would come to relieve him soon. The poor guy looked exhausted, but at least he seemed to be coming around after seeing Jim's death. Vince was worried for a while there, but Bill was more like himself this morning than he had been lately.

Vince was especially glad to see the sun this morning. This was the first time he could see a hint of sky behind the clouds, and the air was definitely improving. There was still a yellowish-brown haze and the occasional column of smoke on the horizon, but it was the best it had been since Sunday. If the weather held, the solar panels might actually draw in enough light to give the batteries a full charge today.

Vince was beginning to feel optimistic about the day as he crossed the street and finished off his cup of coffee. He only hoped the looters stayed away long enough to give them a chance to get something done.

· 18 ·

Vince decided to start another pot of coffee over at the garage. With the sun coming up and the likelihood of the batteries being recharged, he saw no harm in splurging a little and using the coffee maker for a few minutes. Besides, he'd have to use the power anyway if he was going to run the grinder. He wouldn't push his luck, though, and figured on using a generator to power the welder.

He had a few ideas about where to find steel sturdy enough to use as forks on the loader bucket. He had an old pair of rear leaf springs off a one-ton pickup in his yard. They were in a pile of scrap metal destined for the recycler down in Quincy. Thankfully, he hadn't gotten around to hauling it down there yet.

He'd already thought it through, and if the springs were in good enough shape, they just might work. If he could split one side of the spring pack open and drive it onto the front edge of the bucket so that one part of the spring was over and one part was under, they would almost hold themselves on. A little welding for added strength and they'd make a good set of forks for the bucket. They'd also be easy enough to remove later if he wanted to.

He unlocked the garage, and after turning on the breaker that ran the front of the shop, he wasted no time starting the coffee maker. He started for the rear door and stopped as he remembered that it was inoperable from the attempted break-in. He grabbed a hand truck and made his way out the front and around to the yard, wondering if any of the looters were part of the crew that tried to rob the garage. For all he knew, in one of the first encounters he might have already taken out the ones responsible.

He tried to put it out of his mind as he approached the scrap metal pile in the far corner of the fenced-in yard. Fortunately, the set of leaf springs wasn't buried under too much junk, and he had the first one out and free of the pile in no time. As he began to move some junk to get to the other one, he caught a whiff of something foul and it took him a minute to figure out what it was. Then he smelled it again, only it was stronger this time.

"Oh man," Vince muttered. He'd forgotten all about the bodies he and Cy had dumped in the field behind his shop. It wasn't that he'd forgotten about what happened, but more like he'd put it out of his mind. After what these men had put him and the others through, giving them a decent burial wasn't exactly a priority. They killed Jim in cold blood, after all.

But it was time to do something about the three corpses that were quickly rotting beyond the fenced-in yard. With this heat, the stench wasn't going to get any better. It wasn't something he was looking forward to, but at least with the loader he could bury them and keep his distance.

He tried not to look, but curiosity got the best of him, and he glanced back in their direction. He could see the pile of bodies from where he stood, and he quickly looked away when he noticed a raven perched on top of them. The shiny black bird was busy pulling at something that Vince imagined was a piece of intestine.

He forced himself to focus on the task at hand and put his energy into yanking the last leaf spring out from under an old fender. Dragging it away from the pile, he purposefully turned his back to the gruesome scene. He loaded the two sets of leaf springs onto the hand truck and headed for the garage as fast as he could before the wind turned and brought the smell of death with it once again.

Once inside the garage, he looked the spring packs over carefully and was happy to see they were both solid, albeit a little rusty. He'd have to grind them down a bit to expose clean metal and grind off the spring hanger eyes at both ends in order to weld them onto the bucket, but that would be easy enough.

He wiped the sweat away from his face and decided that, before he did anything, he'd have a drink of water and then a fresh cup of coffee. Retrieving the springs from the pile of old parts had taken more out of him than he realized. It was already hot, and the day hadn't even really started yet. He was going to have to pace himself or he'd burn out before accomplishing much of anything today.

He figured he'd probably have to grind the bucket on the loader a little as well, at least in the areas where he was going to attach the springs, but before he did that, he would have to suck it up and bury the bodies. Vince was afraid if he attached the springs first, they would get in the way of digging a hole with the bucket, and he didn't want to risk breaking them off in the ground, either. It was settled, then; that was the next order of business for the morning, like it or not.

With his insulated mug full of coffee and the power turned off at the garage, he locked up and headed for the loader across the street. He was glad to see that Sarah had taken over watch duties for Bill, and he hoped the guy was getting some much-needed rest. He was counting on Bill to put another wheel and tire on the van later in the day. Even though the van had a bad transmission, it was their best bet to transport the livestock from Mary's house back to the motel. Vince knew it would be slow going but hoped to get it done in just two trips. It wasn't like they could go very fast with a van full of animals anyway.

Vince eyed the row of motel room doors and didn't notice any movement. It was still early, and at 6:30 in the morning and after the night they'd had, he wasn't really expecting a lot of activity out of anyone. He climbed into the loader and gave Sarah a nod as he closed the door on the cab. The loader sputtered a few times before the big diesel roared to life. A large puff of black smoke spat out of the rear stack and drifted away in the breeze. Thankful that it started without incident, he raised the bucket and put it in gear.

He headed straight across the street and down the fence line of his property. The crushed-grass tire tracks were still visible from where he and Cy had backed the pickup along the fence and dumped the bodies. He followed the tracks back to where the dead looters were piled up, and now that he was closer, he could see that they were in much worse shape than he anticipated. The bodies were torn up pretty badly, much more than they should have been from simple decomposition. Vince guessed animals were to blame—and more than just a few crows or vultures.

His mind wandered through a short list of predators and scavengers that were native to Indiana. He had seen his share of black bears and coyotes while hunting in the woods, but there were also mountain lions and wolves native to the state. The last two animals were rare, and he had personally never run across a wolf or mountain lion, but he'd heard plenty of stories from some of the older farmers who came into his shop.

Vince first thought to grab a few bucketfuls of dirt and cover the bodies quickly, but he worried that whatever had been feeding on them would return and dig them out. It would be better to dig a deep hole and bury them, so he set about doing just that. He tried not to look at the gruesome pile of flesh and bone; he was glad that nobody was awake yet and here to witness this. With the pit dug, he used the bucket to back-drag the bodies into the hole. He felt like he could feel the remains of the looters through the controls as he operated the bucket. On more than one occasion, he smelled them as well.

Vince finished covering the hastily dug grave with a few bucketfuls of dirt that he then tamped down with the blade. Hopefully this would be enough to keep out any unwanted critters. He turned the loader around and headed back without wasting any more time there.

Survival

He looked over at his garage as he drove down the fence line and thought how strange it was to now have buried bodies in the field behind his shop. No matter what happened in the weeks, months, or years ahead, from this point forward, he would never look out the back door of his place without thinking about what happened here. But the thought quickly paled in comparison to the feeling he got in the pit of his stomach when he looked down the street and surveyed what was left of his once peaceful little town. He would never look at anything in Cloverdale in the same way again, and neither would anyone else.

. 19 .

Vince considered pushing part of the roadblock aside and heading back toward the quarry. They would have to eventually do something with the bodies they had left out on the highway last night. That was the main way into Cloverdale from the interstate, and Vince didn't want any possible survivors to be turned away due to their first impression of the town being rotting corpses along the roadside.

There were bound to be other survivors out there—good people or travelers looking for help or in need of refuge. Maybe even someone or a group that could help Vince and the others in some way. Any survivors coming through here would certainly bypass their town in a hurry if they were greeted by the remnants of last night's skirmish.

Vince sat at the edge of the garage parking lot with the loader halfway onto the street as he mulled over what to do. Maybe he should wait for backup, although he felt more confident during the daylight hours. But it was still risky to go that far from town on his own. He was about to say "screw it" and head for the roadblock when he caught some movement out of the corner of his eye.

It was Cy and Reese. Carrying some of the empty water containers and heading toward him, they crossed the motel parking lot with Reese's dog, Buster, who led the way by a good distance. The energetic yellow lab was undoubtedly enjoying his newfound freedom from the confines of the motel room and running around the parking lot wildly, only stopping long enough to mark the occasional bush or patch of grass.

Vince was jealous of the dog's energy but encouraged by seeing his son and Reese awake and looking to be in good spirits. Seeing the two of them was a good enough excuse for him to abandon his plans to head out and clean up the remaining bodies right now. He gladly cut the wheel, spun the loader around, and headed back to the garage. Vince was anxious to talk to Reese and hear how her dad was doing. It had been on his mind since Fred had gotten sick, and he was genuinely concerned for him. He also wondered what the implications would be for the rest of the group if it was in fact due to radiation sickness.

Vince hadn't had a chance to talk with Reese since her dad took ill and wanted to hear her take on the situation. She might only be a vet student, but she had more medical training than anyone else in the group and he didn't want to discount that. Vince also wanted to discuss the merits of giving everyone another round of potassium iodine tablets.

Vince parked the loader in front of the garage but left the bucket up in the air enough so that he and Cy could add the forks to it. Before he could climb down from the cab, Buster was at the bottom of the ladder, his front paws on the loader as he eagerly waited for Vince to greet him.

"Hey, boy." Vince hopped down, skipping the last step, and answered the dog's plea for attention with a vigorous rubdown. This was enough to convince Buster to remain by Vince's side until Cy and Reese were less than a couple of feet away.

"Morning, Major," Reese said with a slight smile.

"Morning," Vince answered.

"What are you up to with the loader?" Cy asked.

"Oh, just cleaning up a little and getting ready to modify the bucket. I was actually just thinking about coming over to get you and see if you could give me a hand." Vince avoided going into detail and wasn't about to offer up the fact that he had just buried three bodies out back.

"Sure, no problem," Cy said. "We were just coming over to get some water."

"So how's your dad, Reese?" Vince asked.

"He's actually doing much better. He was able to get some sleep last night. I think it's just a stomach thing. Probably just out of sorts from not eating right. It's been a little rough on all of us." Reese rubbed her belly and made a face.

"Yeah, I understand. We're going to try and do something about that today." Vince went into detail about his plans to turn the center courtyard of the motel into a holding pen for Mary's animals. He also explained the need to clear a path to her house. He ran the idea of using the leaf springs as forks for the bucket past Cy, who agreed it would make moving the cars much easier. Cy agreed to help as soon as they had the water containers filled and he helped Reese bring the containers back to the others at the motel.

Under Buster's watchful eye, Vince helped them with the water, and after they had refilled all the containers, they loaded them onto the hand truck. Reese insisted that she could handle them by herself and confidently headed back to the motel with a less excited Buster close behind.

Vince and Cy didn't waste any time and started working on the loader. Vince started modifying the springs, and Cy began grinding away the rust on the two areas of the bucket where they would weld them on. It felt good to be working on something with his son, and it gave Vince a much-needed break from worrying, even if it was only temporary. In just a little over an hour, they had the spring packs welded onto the bucket and ready for action. They stepped back and, over the remainder of the coffee, admired the modification they had made. Vince was pleased with how it turned out, and he was confident that it would make the loader much more efficient at moving cars and debris off the roads.

"Mind if I give it a try?" Cy asked.

"I guess. Just be careful. The forks aren't meant to take the full weight of a car. Just use them to get under it and then angle the bucket back to support the bulk of the weight. You know what I'm saying?" Vince was worried that the forks would break off under the full weight of a vehicle and wanted to make sure Cy understood their function.

Cy rolled his eyes. "I got it, I got it."

Vince headed back to turn the breaker off and heard the loader start up. Cy was still just an overconfident kid in so many ways. It made him worry about his son even more. Vince was once that cocky kid who knew it all, and he made plenty of mistakes because of it. The big difference was that any mistakes made now would be costly and dangerous—maybe even the difference between life and death.

By the time Vince made it back to the front of the garage, Cy was already out on the main street, sizing up the first wreck for removal. Vince watched tentatively and bit his lip as Cy positioned the bucket at a downward angle and slid the makeshift forks under the burned-out vehicle. Once the forks were under and the loader started to push the car forward, he stopped and tilted the bucket back as he lifted.

Vince would have done it a little differently and thought about running over to offer some advice, but before he could move, the car broke free of the pavement with a metallic groan. For a split second, Vince thought the springs had given way, but instead, the bucket kept tilting, the car in its grasp. Cy abruptly stopped the tilting motion, and the car jerked backward and slid down the springs to the bucket. He did it. He had the car cradled and ready to move.

From inside the cab, Cy looked back at Vince and smiled as he shook his fist in triumph. Vince nodded and couldn't help but crack a smile. Their contraption had worked. It was a small victory, but he'd take it. Vince jogged over to the loader as Cy opened the cab door.

"For now, let's just get stuff off the road." Vince did want to build a barricade around the little portion of town they were inhabiting, but right now, he thought it made more sense to clear the roads for ease of travel. The thought of having roads that he and the others could easily use was too appealing to ignore. There were enough running vehicles that they could split up into teams and finish what they had started before the fires drove them to seek shelter. They needed to head back out there and look for survivors and supplies.

· 20 ·

Clearing the road went slowly, and after a couple of hours' time, they had only made it about half a mile into town. It wasn't going as quickly as Vince wanted, but at least it was progress and Cy had even managed to start building the beginnings of a wall with debris and rubble from the fires. As the houses and buildings became denser, it was easy to fill in the gaps in yards and start creating a rough barrier around the part of town they were using.

Near the center of town, they discovered that the small grocery store was still partially intact. It had suffered a lot of damage from the fires, but a portion of it had somehow survived. Vince and Cy investigated the store and found a fair amount of good food left in the place. Of course, all the perishables were long gone, but fortunately, a large portion of the canned food section remained intact. Most of the cans were charred and had lost their paper labels, but they were still sealed.

Now that he knew this was here, Vince regretted not venturing out earlier to look for supplies, but he reminded himself of the conditions they faced during those first few days. It was bad enough on the outskirts of town, where his garage and the motel were located. Attempting to get this close to the center of town any sooner would have been futile. He thought back to how bad it was and the close calls he and Mary had just trying to escape this area.

He and Cy let the others know about their find at the grocery store and they immediately began collecting anything salvageable from the store and taking it back to the motel. Everyone pitched in and helped, and they spent the better part of the day sorting through items and weeding out the good from the bad. Some of the canned goods had gotten too hot and burst, but when all was said and done, they managed to salvage 347 cans of vegetables and other things they began to refer to as mystery meals due to the lack of labeling.

Among the canned goods and partially burned aisles, they also found bread and a good assortment of prepackaged dry goods like rice, beans, and pasta. Half the pet food aisle was spared as well, and while that wouldn't do much for them, it would make Nugget and Buster happy campers. Vince had watched Mary try to feed Nugget a portion of her energy bar and taken note of the little dog's lack of enthusiasm. Buster, on the other hand, seemed more than willing to eat anything Reese was gracious enough to share with him.

By the time they resumed clearing the road, the sun was beginning to set. It was starting to look like they wouldn't get to Mary's today or fix the van. But their efforts were well worth it, considering the haul they had taken in. The canned goods were a godsend, and the boost in morale was evident on everyone's faces. Just the thought of eating something besides an energy bar for dinner was enough to make Vince feel like the day was a success.

After he had finished his turn at standing watch, he took over in the loader for Cy. He glanced at the horizon every so often as he watched the sun sink lower and lower, disappointed to see how fast he was losing daylight. He was tempted to work in the dark but was concerned that the looters would return now that they had the cover of night on their side.

There was strength in numbers, and they all needed to stick together, especially when they were most vulnerable. Also, the ladies had promised to fix a meal for everyone tonight and he wasn't about to miss out on that. It had been a long time since any of them had eaten a hot meal. Sarah and Hannah had proposed the idea as a way to celebrate the food they found today.

And while Vince agreed that they all deserved a good meal, he also wanted to be around to make sure they weren't wasteful. He didn't think they would be, but he was conservative; it was just his way. He knew that finding the supplies was pure luck, and they couldn't count on that happening again. It would be important to make the food last as long as possible. While it seemed like a lot, it would go quickly feeding thirteen people.

Vince waved at John to signal that he was heading back to the motel. John had taken over for Cy and was watching from his Bronco now that it was dark out. They decided to have one man stay near whoever was operating the loader. It was impossible to hear anything over the big machine's diesel engine, and Vince didn't want to get caught off guard if the looters attacked again. It seemed like a waste of manpower, but he had agreed to keep everyone happy and had to admit it probably wasn't a bad idea.

Vince glanced around, surveying the day's efforts, and was pleased with what they had accomplished. He hoped to clear more road than this, but the grocery store more than made up for it. Mary's animals would have to wait one more day. He saw no reason why they shouldn't be able to go out to her place tomorrow.

At this rate, it would be at least another day or so before he could even think about trying to check out what was left of his house. And if he did that, it was only reasonable to expect that the others would want to go back to their homes and assess their losses as well. Most of the group lived in town or close by, except the Morgans.

Reese and her parents lived down near Quincy, and that was a bit of a drive from Cloverdale—about forty-five minutes on a good day. The road to Quincy led south out of town and directly past his place. They should probably travel together for safety and kill two birds with one stone. But there were two things he didn't like about that plan. One, it meant taking time away from the things he needed to do around here. Two, it would leave only a handful of people in town to watch over things.

Vince was okay with leaving John here, but the thought of it still made him nervous. They could be gone for a few hours at least, and the two-way radios wouldn't work over that distance, if yesterday's performance was any indication of their range. If something went down while they were away, they would have no way of knowing until they got back.

Vince began to wonder if they should all stay put until they had the barrier built—or at least most of it. Other than driving out to Mary's and getting the animals, that might be the best thing to do. Of course, the others would have to go along with it, and there had already been talk by some of them about wanting to go to their houses. He was just going to have to convince them otherwise.

Vince looked at his watch as he pulled the loader along the curb in front of the motel. It was nearly 8:30 and already dark out. On a normal June evening, there would have still been enough light out to see without the loader's spotlights. But early darkness was just another reminder that the atmosphere was still thick with smoke and that this was anything but a normal summer evening.

· 21 ·

As badly as Vince wanted to keep working, he had to admit that it felt good to turn the loader off as he stood outside the cab and basked in the quietness of the night. He even felt like the smell of smoke and burnt things had subsided some, but he wondered if maybe he was just getting used to it. Though there were no more raging fires glowing on the horizon like there had been in the beginning, he had noticed smoke still rising from most structures he'd seen today.

The day had been a success by any measure, but it was disheartening to see the extent of the damage and destruction that had turned Cloverdale into a pile of ash and rubble. It was especially hard for Mary to take in what had become of her hardware store. Vince tried to console her as best as he could while they stood in the parking lot, looking over the remains of her building. There wasn't much to be said, and he felt helpless in his efforts to make her feel better.

He thought she handled it well, and all things considered, she was still one of the lucky ones. Not all was lost from her store, and the outdoor section that consisted of a small lumber yard and landscaping section had survived. Once the pile of debris had cooled enough to get in there with the loader and clear a path without the risk of blowing a tire, they could salvage some of the things in her yard.

Fencing and lumber would come in handy and help transform the motel courtyard into a suitable place for holding the animals. And there were gardening supplies and piping that could be used to grow food and run irrigation. Everything they needed was there; they just had to put it to use.

Vince nodded at Cy, who was sitting in the pickup and pulling a watch shift. Cy barely acknowledged him at first due to that fact that he was shoveling food into his mouth from a paper plate.

"They've got food in there, in the back room," Cy mumbled between mouthfuls.

"Thanks," Vince answered.

"How are you? Okay?" Cy asked.

"Yeah, why?" Vince asked without slowing down.

"You're limping a little, that's all."

"Just a little stiff from the loader. I'll be all right." If he was being honest, Vince was more than a little stiff, but there was no point in complaining. The seat in the loader wasn't particularly uncomfortable, but after a few hours behind the wheel, it had worn him out. In fact, he felt like he could still hear the drone of the diesel ringing in his ears and still feel the vibrations of the steering wheel in his fingers. Someone else was going to have to take a turn behind the wheel tomorrow.

Between him and Cy, they had practically run the loader all day and managed to burn through all but a quarter of the fuel. While the forks they made for the loader bucket worked out great for moving vehicles, they weren't as useful at clearing debris from fallen building and houses. Having a pair of removable forks for the bucket would have been nice so that they could easily switch back and forth for certain tasks. Something for Vince to consider, but right now, he couldn't think of anything that would do the trick.

Before they resumed any work, they were also going to have to top off the tank with diesel fuel tomorrow over at his garage. At least there was sunlight for most of the day today, which meant the solar panels had plenty of light to give the reserve batteries a full charge. That meant running the fuel pumps and the well pump in the morning wouldn't be any problem.

Vince had checked all the wrecks they moved today for any salvageable batteries, but they had all melted, and he expected as much. That was all right, though; he figured on getting all the batteries he needed from the Chevy dealership on the other side of town. He'd link as many batteries together as he could and create a huge bank of reserve power—enough to provide electricity to the motel and maybe anything else they needed to run. At least that was the plan; he was no electrician, but he was optimistic that between him and Cy, they could figure out how to make it work.

As Vince headed toward the conference room in the motel, he began to smell something that he hadn't smelled in what seemed like forever. The aroma of hot food hit him like a wave as he opened the door, and his mouth began to water at the sight of the food laid out on the table. Under normal circumstances, it might not have looked like much, but right now, the various plates of vegetables and pasta looked like a smorgasbord. It had been far too long since they'd had a decent meal.

"Help yourself, Major," Bill said. Vince nodded and didn't waste any time grabbing a plate and digging in. The group ate in silence. The only other sound in the small room was the occasional slurping of spaghetti noodles and the gulping of water to wash the food down. Mary took another serving of food out to Cy in the truck before it was gone, and in what seemed like minutes, the table was empty.

They all sat around for a bit after the meal in what Reese jokingly called a food coma. It had been the largest meal any of them had had since last Sunday. Vince hoped they didn't overdo it and worried that maybe it was too much too fast. Only Ryan and Sasha had any visible energy left after eating. They were throwing an empty water bottle down the hallway for Buster and Nugget in a game of fetch. It was the first time that Vince had seen either one of the kids act as children should, and it did his heart good to see them play with the two dogs.

As Buster bounded effortlessly down the hallway, Nugget running alongside him, Vince wasn't sure who was more excited about the arrangement. The big yellow lab was careful to keep the water bottle just out of Nugget's reach but close enough to be a tease. No matter how many times the kids tossed the bottle, neither dog seemed to tire of the game until Buster decided to lie down with his prize and make it a chew toy. Nugget wasn't having it, though, and challenged Buster with a few playful barks and whines before stealing the toy and taking off with it in her mouth. Buster retaliated by chasing Nugget around the room in a comical game of keep-away that had everyone laughing uncontrollably.

They were all thoroughly entertained by the show, and it was a welcome distraction from their lives. It was the first time any of them had laughed in days. And for just a little while, everyone forgot about the tragedy playing out beyond the motel walls.

At least until a long blast from the pickup truck horn cut through the air like a knife and brought the frivolity to an abrupt stop. Even the dogs ceased their antics and stood still as the horn sounded a second time. Vince watched as Nugget twisted her head in an effort to understand the noise, and he forced himself to stand up and reluctantly accept the fact that the looters were back.

· 22 ·

When the realization of what was happening sank in, Vince and the others scrambled for their weapons. Sarah and Beverly rounded up their children and held them close. Reese and Mary joined the men as they made their way toward the front of the motel and the doors that led outside to the parking lot.

"John," Vince said, "let's you and I go see what's going on before we all go running outside. The rest of you wait here and be ready to move when we figure this out." He held the door and let John slip out as he made eye contact with Mary. He could see the concern in her eyes, and understandably so, but she didn't argue with his plan, and neither did anyone else.

Vince and John hustled across the parking lot and made their way to the passenger door of the Ford pickup, where Cy was sitting, binoculars up to his face as he scanned the darkness.

"I saw a light out on the road, past the roadblock, but it went out before I could get a good look with these."

"Was it an ATV or a car? What did it look like?" John asked.

"No, it looked like a flashlight, but I'm not sure." Cy handed the binoculars to his dad.

"Do you think they're trying to sneak in on foot?" Cy glanced at John and his dad before looking back out the truck window.

"Anything's possible with these guys," Vince answered. "They seem pretty determined."

"I guess we better go have a closer look," John said.

"Cy, you stay put. We'll go let the others know what's going on." Vince backed out of the pickup and stayed low as he and John made their way to the motel. Everyone was where they had left them, waiting anxiously to find out why Cy had blown the horn.

"Well?" Mary asked before Vince could say anything.

"Cy thinks he saw a flashlight out past the roadblock," Vince said. "John and I are going to go check it out. It could be nothing."

Bill rubbed at the back of his neck nervously. "Or it could be those same people trying to sneak in close for another attack."

"I'm coming with you," Tom volunteered.

"Fine," John agreed. "Then the three of us will go check it out. The rest of you get into your positions like we talked about."

A couple of days ago, they had all agreed on a plan of sorts for if and when they were attacked again. Whoever was on watch would stay put, and the remaining people would take up predetermined defendable positions around the motel property. The kids and their mothers would barricade themselves into the room with the supplies. Fred would join them. If he was on watch at the time, Bill would go instead.

Vince and John figured they'd rather know where everyone was during an attack rather than have them randomly scattered about. They also had decided to spread out the positions, hoping to give the impression that they had more people than they did. Everyone except the kids had their own weapons now and had been instructed to carry them at all times. Although Vince was reluctant to arm people who had little or no experience with firearms, he decided it was better than being caught unarmed and defenseless.

He and John had given a very brief talk on firearms safety and operation to those who needed it. It was inadequate, and they knew it, but with the amount of ammunition they had, they couldn't afford to have actual, live fire practice. The way things were going, they would need all they had for the real thing.

As everyone began to scatter and take their positions, Vince, John, and Tom made their way toward the street, trying to keep a low profile as they went. John held up the radio and flashed it at Cy in the truck, indicating for him to turn his on. They had been keeping the radios off to conserve batteries—another tough decision that limited their communication abilities, but one that was necessary so they had them for occasions like this.

Vince kept his eyes wide open as he scanned the landscape in front of them and beyond the roadblock for any signs of activity. He led the others single-file as they stayed close to the edge of the motel to hide their profiles. As they left the corner of the building and crossed an open area to a small stand of trees, he was now very thankful for the total darkness. Of course, the darkness worked both ways and made it equally as difficult for them to spot any intruders or potential threats.

They crouched down in the cover of the small pine trees for a couple of minutes and remained silent as they strained to see through the darkness. As Vince's eyes adjusted, he began to make out some familiar outlines of the landscape. He could see the overpass down the road and make out the flat areas of field on either side of the highway.

"Do you think they were coming back for the bodies?" Tom whispered.

"I don't know," John answered. "They don't really seem like the type of people to care about that unless they were looking for the weapons."

"The ones I saw when we were out there were useless," Vince added.

John held the radio close to his mouth. "Come in, Cy. You see anything? Over."

"No, nothing. Over," Cy responded immediately.

"Should we get a little closer or go back?" Tom asked.

Vince looked around and weighed their options. They definitely weren't going back until they figured out what was going on. He believed that Cy had seen something, and it made sense to him. The looters had failed in their previous attempts at coming into town in plain sight, so it was reasonable to assume they would try a different tactic now.

"Well?" Tom whispered a little louder this time, anxious for a plan from either one of them.

From where they were, their view was blocked by a few taller weeds and bushes along with the occasional road sign. "Let's make our way up to the roadblock," Vince suggested. "We'll have a clearer view of the road from there."

John nodded. "Yeah, okay."

Vince led the group again and made his way to the edge of the trees before running in a crouched position into the ditch that ran along the road. They stayed down in the cover of the ditch until they reached the cars Vince had pushed together with the loader. After climbing out the ditch, they positioned themselves behind the roadblock and peered through the burned-out wrecks and at the road beyond.

They sat still for a few minutes, waiting to see if they could pick up any movement, but they saw nothing.

"Now what?" Tom asked.

Vince was growing tired of Tom's impatience. "We wait," he answered firmly. Now it was a game of patience, and whoever made a mistake first would be the loser. Vince got comfortable on the ground and found a spot where he could see around the corner of one of the cars. He thought about all the times he had sat in a deer stand and remained perfectly still while he tried to pick up any movement in the woods. This reminded him a little bit of that. The biggest difference was that he was the one being hunted now.

· 23 ·

Vince could tell that Tom was growing more restless by the minute, and he worried that his constant shifting and fidgeting would give away their location. John must have been thinking the same thing. He told Tom to head back to the motel and that he and Vince would stay put and keep a lookout. Tom agreed and made his way back down the ditch and was soon out of sight.

Vince would usually agree that there was strength in numbers, but this was one time he was glad to have one less. Tom was a good shot with the AR-15 and had proven his value the other night when they retrieved the loader, but he lacked patience. Vince wasn't the most patient person in the world, either, but when it came to this kind of thing, he could control his urges. The last thing he wanted was to blow their cover and lose the advantage they currently had.

As he and John sat there, the clouds gave way,

allowing the pale moonlight to break through and reflect off the pavement. In this moment, he was certain that he spotted two figures walking down the shoulder of the road, just past the overpass. He blinked and rubbed at his eyes, wanting to be certain that the light wasn't playing tricks on his mind.

Vince pointed. "John, over there, do you see it?"

"Yeah, I see it." John propped up his AR-15 with the fixed magnification scope and tried to get a better look. "Two people walking this way. Doesn't look like they're carrying any weapons, but I'm not sure. Hard to tell. They've got some backpacks on, it looks like. I don't think they're part of the gang that's been attacking us." He passed the rifle to Vince so he could look for himself.

Sure enough, Vince made out two figures with bags on their backs. There were no long guns visible, but that didn't mean anything. It was still dark, and as the clouds obscured the moon once more, he all but lost sight of them.

"They're definitely coming this way. I say we stay put and let them come to us. But for right now, I would have to agree that they don't look like they're with the looters." Vince handed the AR back to John.

John pulled out the radio again. "Come in, Cy. We've got eyes on 'em. Two people headed our way. Over."

"Copy that. Just two of them? Over."

"Not sure yet. Stand by. Over." John set the radio down and took another look through his scope. Vince stared off in the direction he had last seen the figures before the moonlight vanished. He wondered who these people could be. It was possible that they were just travelers coming off the interstate. Based on the events of the last few days and the bad guys they'd been dealing with, Vince and the others were more than a little paranoid. And who could blame them? It wasn't like they'd encountered anyone friendly from outside of town so far. Still, though, he was hopeful that these people didn't have anything to do with the gang of looters, although he wasn't about to roll out the welcome mat just yet.

He and John decided to stay put and let them come close enough so they could identify them and get a better look. They also wanted to make sure it wasn't a trap and there weren't more of them lurking in the shadows.

They were close enough now that Vince could hear their footsteps as they approached the roadblock. If they were trying to sneak up on the town, they weren't doing a very good job. He could now make out voices that sounded like a man and a woman, as well as an assortment of other odd noises that sounded like dull clanging.

He was growing more convinced that they were

just a couple of random people coming off I-70. Maybe their car had broken down somewhere. He couldn't imagine where they would be walking from at this hour or why, but he was still suspicious as to why they weren't using the flashlight Cy had seen earlier.

At less than twenty yards away, it was time to make a move. They were clearly on their own, and Vince and John could stop them where they were and still use the roadblock for cover if there were any surprises. John glanced at Vince and signaled that he was ready. They jumped to their feet with their guns at the ready as John called out to the strangers.

"Hold it right there!" The couple froze in their tracks, searching for the source of the voice in the darkness. When they saw Vince and John, they both held their hands up and stepped back a few feet.

"Are you alone?" John barked.

The man stepped in front of the woman. "Ye... Yes it's just the two of us. Our car broke down a few hours ago," the man replied.

Vince looked around to make sure there weren't any other people lurking nearby before he stepped out from behind the roadblock and slowly approached them. John was right behind him, and as soon as they were about ten feet away, Vince turned his flashlight on the couple for a better look.

They looked to be in their thirties. Both carried backpacks loaded down with enough gear to make them bulge at the seams. The water bottles and other stuff hanging from carabineers on the outside of the packs only made them look even more cumbersome. At least he knew what had been making the strange noises he heard as they approached. Neither one appeared to be carrying any type of weapon other than the large black Maglite the man held. The flashlight was large enough to use as a club, but Vince wasn't concerned. The poor guy looked like he was doing all he could just to carry it.

They were both dirty and sweaty, and without question, Vince could easily buy the story about them walking for the last few hours. They looked pretty rough, and their clothes were ripped, but that wasn't unusual, all things considered. They were all looking pretty rough these days, Vince included.

The couple looked scared, and at that moment, he decided to lower his gun. Glancing over at John, he realized that they probably looked fairly intimidating themselves, and from what he could tell so far, the couple didn't seem to pose any immediate threat. John followed suit and lowered his gun as well.

"Where are you guys coming from?" Vince asked.

"Indianapolis," the man answered as he and the woman inched toward the roadblock. John stepped up ahead of Vince and greeted the couple with an outstretched hand.

"The name's John. I'm the sheriff here in town. Well, I mean, I was when we had a town. Not much left now."

"You're still the sheriff." Vince shifted his shotgun to his left hand and offered his other to the couple. "I'm Vince."

"Hi, I'm Dave, and this is my wife, Kelly. We were headed for New Mexico to Kelly's parents' house. They've got a place just outside Santa Fe." Dave paused, looked over at his wife, and smiled weakly at her before continuing. "Not sure if we're gonna make it too much farther without a car, though."

Vince glanced over at John, and he knew what his friend was thinking without John having to say it.

John nodded at Vince. "If you like, you guys can stay here with us until you get things figured out. There are about a dozen of us staying at the motel up the road there. We have some supplies and water, and we can offer you one of the rooms to use."

Kelly let out a deep breath. "Wow, that would be great. Thank you."

"Thanks, we're exhausted. A bed sounds great," Dave added.

"Well, come on, then," Vince said. "Follow us back. It's not safe out here anyway."

"What do you mean by that?" Dave asked.

"We've been having some trouble from a group of looters or a gang. Whatever you want to call them. That's the reason for the roadblock." Vince looked at the pile of cars behind him.

John pulled the radio off his belt and held it up to his face. "Come in, Cy. We met a couple of travelers. We're headed back your way now. Let everybody know everything's okay. Over."

"Copy that," Cy responded. "I'll pass it on to the others. Over."

"We keep a guy on watch at all times," John added. "That's how we knew you guys were coming. Vince's son, Cy, spotted your flashlight."

"Yeah, our batteries died." Dave held the large flashlight up and clicked the button several times.

Vince was a little disappointed that John had readily given up so much information to the new arrivals. Neither one looked dangerous and their story was believable, but Vince thought it was too early to give them any more information than was necessary.

"This gang, they're that big of a problem?" Dave asked.

"Unfortunately yes," John answered. "They killed one of our friends a few days ago. They mean business for sure."

"Oh no." Kelly gasped as she put her hand up to her mouth.

"Yeah, they've forced us to fight back, but we're holding our own," John continued. "It hasn't been easy, but we're armed and ready for them."

Kelly continued to shake her head in disbelief as they began to walk toward town.

"I thought it would be better once we got out of the city," Dave said. "It's bad in Indianapolis. Like, really bad. We took our chances when we found a working car and made a run for it. It's absolute chaos for anyone left alive. There's no food or water left anywhere, and we've been hearing gunshots at all hours of the day and night. It was pretty quiet at first, but things got crazy fast. I guess everyone that survived the initial blast was in shock and stayed hidden indoors initially. I know that's what we did. But the quietness didn't last for long. I think once people realized that there was no help coming, things got a little crazy. It's every man for himself back there." Dave looked at Kelly again. The expression on his face spoke volumes about what they had seen in Indianapolis. Kelly remained silent and looked down at the ground as they walked.

Vince wasn't surprised to hear the news, but getting it firsthand made it real. A small part of him hung on to the hope that the government would step in and send the National Guard or FEMA to try and stabilize the bigger cities, but apparently that wasn't the case. If there was no law and order in Indianapolis and the people there were left to fend for themselves, what did that mean for them here in Cloverdale?

Vince knew what it meant, though, and Dave and Kelly's account of the state of affairs in the city confirmed his worst fears. It meant that things were going to be like this for a while and that, most likely, they were going to be on their own for a very long time.

· 24 ·

Vince glanced behind them, down the road and toward the interstate, but the clouds and smoke had covered the moon completely now. All he could see was a pitch-black void behind them. The darkness made him want to walk faster; being this far from the relative safety of the motel at night made him nervous. They needed their flashlights to see, but the lights also made them an easy target, should anyone be looking.

Dave and Kelly were evidently pushing their limits physically and struggling to keep up with the already slower pace he and John were setting for them. Kelly looked to be suffering the worst. She was walking with a bit of a limp, and if they had been walking for a few hours, she probably had a few blisters. By the looks of it, she might not make it at all if Vince didn't do something.

"Here, let me take your bag for you," Vince offered. Maybe he could speed up the pace if he took her load. He wasn't exactly full of energy, either, but he was willing to suffer a little if it meant they could make better time.

"Oh no, I couldn't. I can manage," Kelly insisted as her foot caught something on the road and she stumbled. Dave managed to grab her arm and catch her before she went down. She looked embarrassed by her clumsiness.

"Come on, really, let me carry it. I don't mind," Vince said.

"Well, okay, maybe just for a minute," she said reluctantly. Vince handed his shotgun to John and helped her unload the large bag from her shoulders. Kelly sighed as she transferred the weight to Vince. No wonder she was exhausted. The bag must have weighed fifty pounds. Vince grunted as he hoisted the backpack onto his shoulders and tried to situate it.

"Sorry about that," she said. "There are some canned goods and the last of the food from our apartment in there. Everything we have left in the world is in these two bags." She tried to laugh, but it sounded more like she was fighting back tears.

Dave put his hand on her shoulder and tried to comfort her. "It'll be all right. We're still alive and we have each other."

Suddenly Vince felt very guilty for holding them at gunpoint a few minutes ago. They were vulnerable and had lost nearly everything, not unlike him and the others back at the motel. They were just trying to survive this nightmare that had become their lives.

Vince took his gun back from John, and they resumed walking, this time at a slightly faster pace. The bag was heavy and cut into his shoulders; he couldn't imagine how she had made it so far with this burden. At least the motel wasn't far now, and he felt better being a little ways past the roadblock. They continued on in silence until the radio crackled and Cy's voice came over the speaker.

"Come in, guys. Are you sure there's only two of them? Over."

John grabbed the radio off his belt again. "Go ahead, Cy. What are you saying now? Over."

"I see lights behind you," Cy answered. "Looks like they're coming from near the overpass. Over."

They all froze mid-step and turned to look toward the interstate. Vince stared in disbelief as his brain registered what was unmistakably a pair of headlights coming straight at them. He knew in his gut that it was the looters this time. They had pushed their luck being out here like this, and now it had run out.

Who else could be coming from that direction and at that speed? The flashlights had given them away. Either that or the looters were just coming to do what they had done so many other nights and Vince and the others were just plain unlucky enough to be caught out here.

Vince glanced back at the motel. They were still a couple of hundred yards away. He looked at John and then back at the quickly approaching vehicle. Could they make it if they ran? Even if he and John could, Dave and Kelly wouldn't be able to do it, even if Dave dropped the bag. He couldn't just leave them behind; they'd be as good as dead if they were caught.

Vince wasn't sure if the looters could force their way past the roadblock with their car, but they were crazy enough to try it. The burned-out wrecks were nothing more than skeletons of vehicles and weren't that heavy. The more he thought about it, the more he questioned the roadblock's ability to stop a high-speed impact if they decided to ram their way through. And if they didn't ram it, they could stop at the roadblock and shoot at them from there. There was no good cover between here and the motel. Vince didn't want to get caught out in the open, running for his life.

Vince let Kelly's bag slide off his back and fall to the ground. "Run! Drop your bag and run."

Dave glanced around nervously for a second. Vince was afraid he wasn't going to leave the bag at first, but he finally gave in. His heavy backpack hit the pavement with a *thud* as he grabbed Kelly's hand and pulled her toward the motel.

"Don't wait for us. We'll hold them off!" Vince shouted. He stood there for a minute, weighing his options. The roadblock wasn't that far behind them and would provide good cover. Their only other choice was to get into one of the ditches, but they wouldn't have a good vantage point from there until the car was practically on top of them.

"Ditch or roadblock?" John asked. At least he was on the same page as Vince.

"Roadblock. We can make it there before they get to us—maybe even stop them before they get too close." Leaving the backpacks on the road, they ran as fast as they could toward the car and the roadblock, then took up positions on either end. Vince chambered a double-aught buckshot shell and prepared to fire. Unfortunately, he had to wait until the approaching car was in range. He didn't want to risk wasting the ammo on a long shot.

The car was still a hundred yards or more out and appeared to have slowed its advance somewhat. The looters were still out of range for Vince's shotgun, and he would have to wait a little longer to fire. He glanced back to see how far Dave and Kelly had managed to run and was disappointed to see they hadn't covered as much ground as he'd hoped. The two weary travelers definitely wouldn't have made it in time. Standing their ground here was the right choice, albeit a dangerous one.

Even though John was on the other side of the roadblock and a good twenty feet away, Vince was still startled by the first sharp crack of the AR-15.

SURVIVAL

The car's trajectory remained unchanged, and John fired again. This time he let loose a volley of four rounds in short succession, each less than a second apart. Vince kept count as he watched the muzzle flash light up the road in front of them and the headlights begin to weave back and forth across the road. That was five rounds spent out of John's thirty-round magazine. Hopefully John was keeping track of his ammo as well. That was the only magazine he was carrying, and Vince knew that he was limited to the shells in his shotgun, regretting now that he hadn't grabbed a few more and put them in his pocket before they left.

It was hard to tell if any of the shots had made contact or if the looters were just taking evasive maneuvers. Either way, they were almost in range of Vince's shotgun.

POP! POP!

John fired two more quick shots from the AR, and one of the headlights disappeared in the darkness. The car swerved hard to the left and stopped broadside to the roadblock at a distance of about seventy yards. It was farther than Vince wanted to attempt a shot with the shotgun, but he began to think that he might not have a choice. It was clear they intended on setting up there for a gunfight.

He watched as three figures scrambled out of the car on the far side and disappeared behind it.

Vince saw the flash of light a split second before the pavement in front of the roadblock erupted in a spray of asphalt particles and dirt that rained down on top of the roadblock. He wasn't sure what they were shooting, but it must have been a high-powered rifle of some type. The chunk of pavement the round removed from the road was substantial, and Vince imagined the next one would have little trouble penetrating the car he was hiding behind.

Thank God the looters were shooting blindly and had nothing solid to zero in on. Still, Vince decided to change locations just in case they had seen his hiding spot. John moved toward the center of the roadblock as well, and they met in the middle. Vince had configured the cars nose to nose, not on purpose, but he was glad he had now. From this position, at least they had the extra protection of the engine blocks.

"I don't know what they have, but it's heavy," John said.

"I agree. Let's hope they only have one of whatever it is. We should be okay here behind the engines, but I still feel exposed." Vince looked down at the bottom of the cars and regretted not adding more debris to the roadblock. One of the looters' bullets could easily ricochet off the pavement and get at them from underneath. It was never his intention to end up pinned down behind the temporary roadblock and he wanted the cars to be easy to move, but in hindsight, he should have made it more permanent.

"I don't want to waste ammo shooting at their car," John said.

"I hear you, and they're a little far for the shotgun." Vince shook his head. Just then another loud shot rang out as the bullet slammed into one of the cars and made a loud metallic *bang*. Then another shot, and a few seconds later another shot, both of which hit the roadblock with loud *bangs*. Apparently, the looters weren't worried about conserving ammunition as much as he and John were.

"We've got to do something," Vince said as he ducked at the sound of yet another incoming bullet. "We can't just sit here all night getting shot at. Sooner or later, they're gonna get lucky."

"I know, I know. I'm thinking," John answered. Out of what Vince could only imagine was frustration, John peeked over the edge of the hood with the AR and fired two rounds back at the looters. Vince reluctantly followed his lead and fired the double-aught buckshot at their assailants. He hated to spend the ammunition without having a concrete target to aim for, but it was satisfying to fight back. He was rewarded for his efforts with the sound of shattered glass, and although he doubted any real damage was done, he hoped it would at least put the looters off taking another shot for a while—maybe long enough for them to figure out a plan.

Vince was mad at himself for getting pinned down here, and as much as he didn't want to do it, he was going to have to ask for help from the others. There was no way he was calling his son to join him in a gunfight. He'd rather die right here than put Cy at risk.

· 25 ·

As Vince squatted there on the ground and tried to think of a way out of this, he couldn't help but wonder if Dave and Kelly really were who they said they were. The looters had never attacked in such a small group before. As far as he could tell, there were only three in the car—maybe four if he had missed one of them, which he easily could have. But still, they normally came with a larger group. Of course, by Vince's count, they had taken out eight of the gang members so far. Maybe there weren't that many of the looters left, although the thought gave Vince little comfort as the bullets continued to sail overhead.

Was it possible that Dave and Kelly were bait to draw them out and lower their defenses? He tried to shake the thought from his mind, but he kept coming back to it. Maybe they should have checked their bags. He and John had just sent two strangers back to the motel without knowing really anything about them.

Knowing they had left their backpacks behind, without hesitation for the most part, gave Vince a little peace of mind. If this was all a ruse, they would have insisted on taking the bags with them—or would they? They could have been hiding weapons under their clothes. His gut told him they were being honest about who they were and their circumstances, but he couldn't stop questioning the decision to send them ahead. He didn't know what to think anymore.

All that had happened in the last few days had made him overly cautious, and it was pushing him to assume the worst about people. He was tired, and on top of that he was irritated that they were having to deal with the looters again. It had been such a good day, all things considered. He was feeling somewhat positive after dinner tonight, like everything was going to somehow work out.

Just then another bullet struck the car, and he felt the vibrations ripple through the thin metal of the fender he was leaning against.

John shook his head. "We have to try to get out of here. We can't sit here all night, trading lead with these idiots."

"I know, and as much as we need help, it won't do us any good to have anybody else get stuck here with us." Vince looked back to check on Dave and

Kelly's progress and saw that they were, for better or worse, out of sight and presumably at the motel. He was about to suggest that they make a break for the ditch on their right and then the thin wood line beyond that when he heard a familiar sound. He and John glanced at each other with the same puzzled look on their faces.

"Is that the loader I hear?" John asked.

"Sounds like it." Vince strained to see into the darkness but couldn't find any sign of the large machine.

Cy's voice crackled over the radio. "Where are you guys exactly? Over."

"Were pinned down behind the roadblock, taking fire. Over," John answered.

"Stay put. We're coming to get you out of there. Over." Vince could hear the loader in the background over Cy's voice. What did he mean "we," and what was he thinking bringing the loader out here? Vince grabbed the radio out of John's hand without saying a word.

"Cy, this is your dad. Do not come out here. We can get out of this on our own." Vince spat the words out as fast as he could. First and foremost, he didn't want to risk Cy getting hurt. Secondly, if something happened to the loader, they'd be back at square one.

"I'm not leaving you out there," Cy answered. "We're on our way. Over."

"Cy, no. I forbid—" Another round struck the roadblock with a loud bang, and Vince ducked and let go of the button on the radio. This time, the bullet penetrated the car and blew through the passenger door panel a few feet away from Vince's head. The thin metal skin peeled back around the oversized exit hole. Within a few seconds of each other, two more shots rang out from what sounded like small-caliber weapons. Great, they were all shooting now.

John grabbed Vince's arm. "I know you're worried about your son, but we need help or we're not getting out of this."

"I know, I know." It wasn't what Vince wanted to hear, but John was right. It was a good thirty-yard run to the woods, and they had to traverse the ditch to get there. The ditch would provide cover, but when they came up the far side, they would be completely exposed all the way to the trees. To make matters worse, the clouds and smoke had given way to the moon once more, giving the looters an even greater advantage. They'd never make it to the sparse cover of the wood line—at least not both of them.

Vince let out a deep breath as he came to terms with the reality of the situation and accepted the fact that his son was coming to their rescue and driving straight into a firefight. He peered over the hood of the car and tried to catch a glimpse of the looters. He hated sitting here and not doing anything to fight back, but the practical side of him knew that using the shotgun at this range was a waste.

"I'll save the rest of my ammo for when they get here," John said. "Then we'll make a break for it." Vince didn't answer and just nodded as another volley of bullets hit the roadblock. This time one of them sailed high overhead, whistling as it passed, but Vince was too worried about Cy to pay much attention to the barrage of gunfire.

"At least Cy's not alone. He did say 'we.'" John tried to reassure Vince, but it did little to ease his mind.

The loader would be a big target, and even if Cy had someone providing cover fire, the chances for a hit were high. The tires, in particular, were one of Vince's bigger concerns. If the looters managed to shoot a hole in one of the tires, they would be in trouble. It wasn't like he had any extra tires that size lying around the shop. They'd have to go back to the quarry and find a replacement off one of the other machines. Even then, there was no guarantee they would find a wheel with the right bolt pattern.

There was also the mechanics of the loader to consider. It was a big target, and while the bucket and the frame itself were made from thick enough steel to repel the onslaught of bullets, the same couldn't be said for the hydraulic lines and engine components. His garage wasn't equipped to work on construction equipment like the loader, and he certainly wouldn't have the parts.

Vince heard the loader as it got closer, and his greatest concern rushed at him like a ton of bricks: the looters were going to start shooting at Cy. The glass-enclosed cab wouldn't provide any measure of safety, and Cy would be completely exposed up that high. Vince wanted to say something to his son over the radio, but he couldn't think of a single thing to tell him right now that would make a difference.

"Oh, great. More looters." John sank down from where he had been peering over the roadblock and leaned against the wheel.

Vince carefully looked over the hood and saw another vehicle pull up behind the car. It looked like a pickup truck, but he couldn't see well enough to tell how many people were inside or what type of truck it was. He quickly ducked behind the hood before the looters decided to shoot again. The situation was getting worse by the minute. He wasn't crazy about Cy coming to get them, but since he insisted, Vince wished he would hurry up before it was too late.

· 26 ·

"This just keeps getting better and better, huh?" Vince assumed the worst and figured that the truck held at least two more looters. There seemed to be an endless supply, and that was probably one of the reasons they kept attacking with such tenacity. A group of people like that would need a lot of supplies to survive. And while Vince was sure they also wanted revenge, he was beginning to realize that they were more interested in their provisions. How much more determined would the looters be if they knew about the food he and the others had lucked into today at the grocery store?

Another gunshot and hard hit to the car brought Vince back to the current situation. The loader was close, and he could clearly hear the clatter of the powerful diesel engine now. Cy was obviously running without the lights, and Vince was grateful for that much. At least they would be somewhat camouflaged in the darkness.

The loader was still a large target and would draw fire when the looters saw it. When it happened, Vince and John would have to capitalize on that moment. He and John stayed low and watched with anticipation as the loader neared. Vince strained to see into the darkness, trying to pick out the silhouette of the large machine, and was eventually rewarded for his efforts. He saw the bucket first, high up in the air and blocking his view of the enclosed cab and Cy, who he assumed was driving. The bucket was tilted back and high enough that he couldn't see inside it.

"Get ready." Vince glanced at John, who was clutching his AR and looked ready to make a run for it. The loader quickly closed the last ten yards or so to the roadblock, and Vince and John didn't move until the bucket was nearly over their heads.

"Now!" Vince heard a voice call out from what sounded like inside the bucket. A split second later, Tom and Fred popped up from their hiding spots inside the bucket and unleashed a barrage of covering fire at the looters.

Vince and John didn't waste any time and sprinted to the loader as Fred and Tom's AR-15s rattled off round after round. Vince cringed with the thought of all the ammunition they were going through, not that they had much of a choice in the matter. At least it seemed to be working, and for the time being, there were no incoming shots, as far as he could tell.

Fred and Tom wouldn't be able to maintain this rate of fire for long, though, and they needed to escape while they had the upper hand. Vince and John both climbed the ladder and found a place to hang on behind the cab and in line with the cover of the heavy steel bucket.

"Hang on!" Cy nodded at them through the glass and threw the loader into reverse. The big John Deere lurched backward awkwardly, and Vince almost dropped his shotgun as they gained momentum. Tom and Fred's cover fire ceased, and Vince wondered if it was by choice or if they had finally run out of ammunition. At the rate they had been shooting, he was afraid it was the latter.

As they backed away from the roadblock, there was no sound but the roar of the diesel and the whine of the gearbox. In reverse, Cy was pushing the loader to its limit at this speed, and Vince was worried the tricky steering would get away from him. But he held it steady and they continued to back away from the roadblock and the looters.

Vince was hopeful that Tom and Fred had taken out a few more of the gang members or maybe even convinced them to abort their attack for the night. But his optimism was quickly shattered when the large steel bucket rang out with a loud gong like an oversized bell as the loader began to take return fire. The incoming shots increased in frequency until the constant plinking of bullets into metal reminded Vince of a hail storm battering a car.

Tom and Fred hastily sank back down behind the protective front edge of the bucket and disappeared once again. Vince closed his eyes as he hung on precariously to his spot behind the cab. They were protected by the thick steel of the bucket, but he worried about the loader itself taking damage. Fortunately, they were still moving backward, away from the looters, and, with each passing second, farther into the darkness and out of sight. The bullets began to wiz by and hit the ground around them, and as they retreated, fewer and fewer bullets stuck the loader.

Eventually, the shooting stopped, and it appeared to Vince that they had made it far enough away to be out of immediate danger. He knew how sensitive the articulated steering was and worried it would get away from Cy as they flew backward down the road in total darkness. He and John weren't in the best positions and were doing their best to hang on as it was. A sharp turn at this speed would surely throw them both from the machine. Vince pictured falling off and being run over by the oversized knobby tires and didn't dare release his grip on the cab to wipe at the sweat that stung his eyes.

SURVIVAL

Vince rapped on the glass enclosure with the butt of the shotgun and attempted to get Cy's attention. "I think you can turn it around now." There was no need to push their luck or the mechanical abilities of the loader now that they were out of range.

It took Cy a second to acknowledge his dad, and Vince could see by the wide-eyed look on his face that he was still operating on pure adrenaline. He needed to calm his son down before he made a mistake and cost them all.

"Cy, it's okay. You can slow down. You did it. We're safe for now," Vince yelled through the glass. Finally, Cy appeared to snap out of his adrenaline-fueled focus and heed his father's warning. The whir of the big knobby tires began to slow, and the loader eased to a more manageable speed. Cy cut the wheel and spun the machine around to face the town before picking up speed again.

Now that they were running forward, Vince could immediately feel the increased stability in the handling of the loader, and he was able to relax his death grip on the corner of the cab. He looked behind them, searching for any signs of the looters. He doubted they were going to give up so easily. After all, they had Vince and the others on the run, and he was sure they would attempt to chase them back to town. It would take the looters some time to get through the roadblock, but they were determined, so it wouldn't stop them completely.

This had been the most aggressive attack yet and certainly displayed the looters' lack of concern for ammunition use. The gang might not have cared or maybe lacked the foresight to realize they would eventually run out, but Vince thought it had more to do with their desperation to obtain more food and supplies. If they could hold the looters at bay for a few more days, maybe the problem would take care of itself. The lack of food alone would have a huge impact on their abilities. If they ran out of supplies, they wouldn't have the numbers or the strength to continue attacking like this.

Of course, none of this really mattered right now, and as the motel and his garage began to take shape in the darkness up ahead, Vince's thoughts returned to their current situation and he began to think of a plan.

"We need to spread out," Vince shouted over the noisy engine. "If they decide to follow us, we can't make it easy on them." John nodded, and Vince tapped on the glass with his shotgun again. He felt the loader slow down as Cy turned to look at him. "Stop here," Vince yelled. Cy continued to slow the loader until it came to a sudden stop along the side of the road. Vince and John climbed down and motioned for Cy to lower the bucket.

Cy popped the cab door open as the bucket descended. "What's the plan? Are they following us?"

"I'm not sure, but we need to be ready for them if they do," John answered.

Tom climbed out of the bucket. "Just let us know what you want us to do. We're ready."

"I'm out of ammo." Fred shrugged and handed the AR-15 to Cy, who passed Fred his 12-gauge shotgun in exchange.

"Why don't you go and park the loader out of sight over there and then go and reload while the rest of us take our positions," Vince said.

John threw Cy the keys to his room. "I've got a full can of .223 in my room. Fill your mag and lock up when you're done."

"Where are the newcomers, Dave and Kelly?" Vince asked.

Fred coughed. "Back at the motel with the others. They looked pretty worn out."

"Dave told us what was going on, and that's when Cy came up with the idea to use the loader to come and help you guys," Tom added.

John nodded. "And we're grateful for that."

"I guess this is going to be a never-ending fight with these guys, huh?" Fred asked.

Vince shook his head. "I'm afraid so, and I don't even think it's about our supplies at this point, at least not completely."

"What's the deal with the new people?" Fred asked. "We didn't get a chance to talk much before we took off in the loader."

John cleared his throat. "They're from Indy, and according to them, it's a war zone. Every man for himself."

"Well I guess we should consider ourselves lucky, then," Cy added.

"It ain't exactly summer camp around here," Tom scoffed. Vince glanced nervously out into the darkness, toward the interstate. There would be time for talk later. He was anxious to get everyone hidden and in position.

· 27 ·

"We can talk later," Vince said. "Right now, we need to get ready in case the looters haven't had enough for one night." Everyone approved and headed out to their positions. Fred agreed to let the others know what was going on before he and Tom took one of the radios and headed back on foot to the motel, where they would assume their posts.

Cy drove the loader back over to the motel and parked it along the curb before heading to John's room to reload his AR-15. He was to be hidden somewhere near the loader at all times. The big machine had proven to be a useful weapon against the looters, and Vince wanted him ready to fire it up and swing into action if need be.

He also had a somewhat selfish motive for assigning Cy that responsibility, but he didn't dare share it with anyone when they had discussed who would go where in case of an attack. He figured Cy was probably safest inside the loader. With everyone shooting at the looters, they would be too distracted to get off a good shot at him. And based on what had just happened, he was confident that it was a good choice.

Vince looked back to verify everyone was moving according to plan as he and John headed over to the garage. Vince took cover behind a pile of tires and empty steel drums that he had roughly assembled the other day. He'd built the small bunker near the front corner of the storefront and situated it between the building and an air fill station on the side of the lot. It was set a few feet back from the corner of the garage, and he was satisfied it would pass for nothing more than a pile of junk to the casual observer, giving him the opportunity to launch a surprise attack or defend himself and the garage from a second position if need be.

Vince had relinquished his rooftop position to John on account of him having the better rifle for the location. The fixed magnification scope he had mounted to his AR-15 wasn't very powerful, but it was still strong enough to see the motel parking lot across the street. The AR-15 wouldn't be as accurate as Bill's .308 deer rifle with the higher-powered scope, but the AR was a semi-auto and better equipped to keep the looters on their toes, should the need arise.

After their first encounter with the looters, Vince

thought it was better to have Bill stationed a little farther away from the potential action. He still seemed a little off to Vince, and he didn't want to risk him freezing up in a critical position. Bill was a good man, and Vince didn't fault him for not being cut out for this type of thing. Not everyone was.

Rather than risk burning Bill out and having him shut down completely, Vince thought it best to play it safe. Bill's talents were in his mechanical ability, and it was better to keep him level-headed and out of the action if possible so he would be ready and capable of helping out with the many projects that lay ahead.

As Vince sat tucked away behind his roughly fortified position, he thought about all they needed to do in the next couple of days. He was focused on moving the animals from Mary's, provided they were still alive. But after tonight's events, he wasn't so sure now and wondered if they shouldn't rethink their priorities. They had burned through a lot of their ammunition in the past few days, and tonight hadn't helped any.

He hated the thought of it, but maybe they should split up tomorrow. It was a greater risk, but the reward could be worth it if they could accomplish more. Getting to his house—or what was left of it—and retrieving his guns and ammunition from the safe was suddenly at the top of Vince's list.

Mary was more than capable, and if Reese and Cy went with her, they should be able to gather the animals. If any of them were injured, who better to help out than Reese? Some of the others could stay behind and start working on setting up the motel courtyard to contain the livestock. If they started early tomorrow, maybe it would be ready by the time they brought the animals back.

Vince could start clearing a path to the rear yard of what was Mary's hardware store so they could access fencing and building materials. That shouldn't take too long, and it should be cool enough now not to risk damaging the loader. There was still smoke rising from the rubble, but he hadn't seen any actual flames today when he was near there.

From there, he could continue on to Mary's house, clearing a path as he went. He wouldn't worry about using the cars and debris that he moved and would instead just focus on pushing it off the road for now. Mary, Reese, and Cy could follow behind him in the pickup. Mary had reminded Vince the other day that they wouldn't need the van to move the animals since she had an old horse trailer that could hold them all. Between the trailer and the pickup, they could gather up the animals and any other supplies they needed from her house.

From Mary's, he could head to his place and

assess the damage. If his house had burned down, he would need the loader to dig the safe out from underneath what was left of it. And even if the house was still standing, he would need the loader because he planned to bring the safe back to the motel. There was a long section of tow chain with hooks on both ends in the garage, and he could use it to haul the safe up and out of the basement. The loader would have no trouble moving the safe to where he could get under it with the bucket.

If he could pull it off, Vince thought it would be worth the risk. It couldn't hurt to have a place to securely lock up ammo and extra guns. After meeting Dave and Kelly tonight, he was certain more survivors would trickle in from either the freeway or town. Not everyone they met could be trusted. He wasn't even sure about Dave and Kelly, and they couldn't afford to risk making themselves any more vulnerable than they already were.

As Vince sat there on an old plastic bucket and peered through the cracks in the tires, waiting for round two from the looters, he thought about how his perception of people had changed since the nukes hit. He liked to think that he was the type of person who was willing to give people the benefit of the doubt. But he could feel that fundamental belief and optimism about strangers quickly eroding. He could easily see the feeling developing into paranoia if it wasn't kept in check. Were the other survivors struggling with these thoughts like he was? He was sure that they were. How could they not after what they'd been through?

They had all been shot at and had witnessed the death of one of their own. Jim was shot down in cold blood and without hesitation by a group intent on taking the very supplies they needed to survive. Every single one of them had lost family members and relatives because of the bombs. And then there were people like John, who had lost everything. Vince glanced up at the roof but couldn't see anything from where he was tucked away.

Poor John. The man had nothing left of his pre-EMP life. His wife and kids were dead and their home burned to the ground. For the first couple of days after he had pulled into town, Vince worried that he had lost John. It was touch and go for a while there, and being trapped in their rooms for days on end wasn't exactly a morale-booster. But John was coping with it somehow and seemed a little better each day. Still, Vince had no illusion that it wasn't tearing John apart on the inside, and he wished there was something more he could do, but what?

John's situation made Vince all the more grateful for his son's safety, and there wasn't an hour that passed by when he didn't thank God Cy's plane landed ahead of schedule. He wondered if he would have even had the will to go on living knowing his son had died. Would he have been able to hold it together and be strong like John? Maybe he could have done it for Mary's sake. He shook the thought from his mind. There was no point in worrying about what-ifs. Cy was safe, and he planned on keeping it that way.

Vince adjusted himself on the hard bucket and checked his watch. His back was long past sore, and his unforgiving plastic seat wasn't helping. It had been a good twenty minutes since their firefight at the roadblock. He scanned the motel parking lot for any sign of movement from the others. He was sure they were growing impatient as well. Maybe the looters had enough for one night. Vince and his group did go at them pretty hard and probably surprised them with their ability to fight back, although it had cost ammunition to make that impression. Vince took some comfort in the fact that the looters had used a fair amount of ammunition as well.

He checked his watch again impatiently and then looked back in the direction of the roadblock, straining hard to pick out some detail in the darkness beyond. Occasionally, the moonlight broke free of the smoke and clouds, playing tricks on his eyes as the line between reality and his imagination began to blur. He was about to give up, come out from behind his bunker, and check in with John to see if he'd seen anything, but he heard yelling from across the street. He looked to see what all the commotion was about and spotted Tom, Fred, and a few others running out into the motel parking lot.

What in the world were they doing? Vince glanced back toward the roadblock, wondering if he had missed something, but there was still no sign of activity.

"Vince!" The sound of John's voice caught him off guard, and it took him a minute to realize that it was coming from above. John was leaning over the edge of the roof, peering down at him with a concerned look on his face.

"Yeah, what's going on?" Vince strained his neck as he looked up at John, his heart rate already increasing in anticipation of what news John had.

"They took Ryan!" John answered.

"What? What do you mean they took Ryan? Who?" Vince didn't understand what was going on.

"The couple, Dave and Kelly—or whoever they really are. They took Tom and Beverly's boy. Hang on. I'm coming down." John's words still weren't making sense to Vince, or maybe he just didn't want to accept what John was telling him. Vince came out from behind the tires as the others continued to gather in the motel parking lot. He could hear Beverly screaming and crying from all the way over at the garage.

John came running around the corner of the building, breathing heavily and wheezing from his hasty descent from the roof. The air quality had improved, but it was still difficult to take a deep breath without feeling the urge to choke.

"The two travelers, they kidnapped Ryan. Held everyone at gunpoint and tied them up. That's all I know. Come on." John motioned for Vince to follow him as he coughed and tried to catch his breath. Then he started for the motel and the group of people who had gathered in the parking lot.

When they reached the small group, Mary was holding a quiet but sobbing Beverly in her arms. Tom was now the one making noise as he stomped about, cursing and making threats out loud.

"I'm going to kill them!" Tom growled through clenched teeth. The others stood around, watching him pace. Fred tried to calm him, but Tom wasn't having it.

"What happened?" Vince interrupted as Tom launched into another tirade of threats aimed at the looters and the two who had taken his son—who Vince was convinced were one and the same.

"They caught us off guard," Mary said. "I guess they were hiding weapons. Both of them had pistols and held us at gunpoint. They said if we wanted to see the boy again that we were to bring all of our supplies to the overpass by tomorrow night and leave them there." Beverly began sobbing louder again as Mary delivered the news.

Tom continued to pace, but now he was quiet, although his bright red face indicated that he was on the verge of exploding.

"I found them tied up with tape over their mouths." Fred held a neatly wound bundle of Paracord in his hand. Vince was still in shock that this had happened right under their noses and even more disappointed that they had fallen for the trap. He wanted to kick himself for not trusting his gut about Dave and Kelly, although he doubted those were their real names.

"We can't give them our supplies," John stated. Beverly stopped crying and pulled away from Mary to look at John.

"They'll kill Ryan if we don't do what they want!" she shouted. But John was right: they couldn't hand over all their supplies to the looters. It would mean certain death for all of them. Without food, they would starve and lose the ability to fight back, and eventually the looters would kill them all. Vince had no doubt that the looters' ultimate plan was to eliminate him and the other survivors. After the deaths of so many of their gang, they would show no mercy to Vince or anyone else in his group.

There was really no choice in the matter, and as he looked around at the others, he knew they were all thinking the same thing. Everyone wanted to get

Ryan back safe and sound, but giving this band of criminals-turned-kidnappers what they wanted was suicide. Vince looked over at John and then at Cy. They both nodded as though they could tell what he was thinking. Vince reached out and grabbed Tom's arm as he marched by, stopping him in his tracks.

"They've got my boy, Major." Tom struggled to say the words clearly, glancing at his wife and then back at Vince.

"I promise you we'll get Ryan back, but we're not giving up any supplies to do it."

Find out about Bruno Miller's next book by signing up for his newsletter:
http://brunomillerauthor.com/sign-up/

No spam, no junk, just news (sales, freebies, and releases). Scouts honor.

Enjoy the book?
Help the series grow by telling a friend about it and taking the time to leave a review.

ABOUT THE AUTHOR

BRUNO MILLER is the author of the Dark Road series. He's a military vet who likes to spend his downtime hanging out with his wife and kids, or getting in some range time. He believes in being prepared for any situation.

http://brunomillerauthor.com/

https://www.facebook.com/BrunoMillerAuthor/

Made in the USA
Lexington, KY
13 June 2019